Jennie Lucas

A REPUTATION FOR REVENGE

PRINCES
Untamed

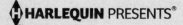

HARLEQUIN PRESENTS®

Recycling programs
for this product may
not exist in your area.

ISBN-13: 978-0-373-23894-1

A REPUTATION FOR REVENGE

Printed in U.S.A.

www.Harlequin.com

All about the author...
Jennie Lucas

JENNIE LUCAS had a tragic beginning for any would-be writer: a very happy childhood. Her parents owned a bookstore, and she grew up surrounded by books, dreaming about faraway lands. When she was ten, her father secretly paid her a dollar for every classic novel (*Jane Eyre, War and Peace*) that she read.

At fifteen, she went to a Connecticut boarding school on scholarship. She took her first solo trip to Europe at sixteen, then put off college and traveled around the United States, supporting herself with jobs as diverse as gas station cashier and newspaper advertising assistant.

At twenty-two, she met the man who would become her husband. For the first time in her life she wanted to stay in one place, as long as she could be with him. After their marriage, she graduated from Kent State University with a degree in English, and started writing books a year later.

Jennie was a finalist in the Romance Writers of America's Golden Heart contest in 2003 and won the award in 2005. A fellow 2003 finalist, Australian author Trish Morey, read Jennie's writing and told her that she should write for Harlequin Presents. It seemed like too big a dream, but Jennie took a deep breath and went for it. A year later Jennie got the magical call from London that turned her into a published author.

Since then, life has been hectic, juggling a writing career, a sexy husband and two young children, but Jennie loves her crazy, chaotic life. Now if she can only figure out how to pack up her family and live in all the places she's writing about!

For more about Jennie and her books, please visit her website at www.jennielucas.com.

Other titles by Jennie Lucas available in ebook:

Harlequin Presents®

3062—A NIGHT OF LIVING DANGEROUSLY
3085—TO LOVE, HONOR AND BETRAY
3116—DEALING HER FINAL CARD (*Princes Untamed*)

CHAPTER ONE

TWO DAYS AFTER Christmas, in the soft pink Honolulu dawn, Josie Dalton stood alone on a deserted sidewalk and tilted her head to look up, up, up to the top of the skyscraper across the street, all the way to his penthouse in the clouds.

She exhaled. She couldn't do this. *Couldn't.* Marry him? Impossible.

Except she had to.

I'm not scared, Josie repeated to herself, hitching her tattered backpack higher on her shoulder. *I'd marry the devil himself to save my sister.*

But the truth was she'd never really thought it would come to this. She'd assumed the police would ride in and save the day. Instead, the police in Seattle, then Honolulu, had laughed in her face.

"Your older sister wagered her virginity in a poker game?" the first said incredulously. "In some kind of lovers' game?"

"Let me get this straight. Your sister's billionaire ex-boyfriend *won* her?" The second scowled. "I have real crimes to deal with, Miss Dalton. Get out of here before I decide to arrest *you* for illegal gambling."

Now, Josie shivered in the cool, wet dawn. No one was coming to save Bree. Just her.

She narrowed her eyes. Fine. She should take responsibility. She was the one who'd gotten Bree into trouble in the first place. If Josie hadn't stupidly accepted her boss's invitation to the poker game, her sister wouldn't have had to step in and save her.

Clever Bree, six years older, had been a childhood card prodigy and a con artist in her teens. But after a decade away from that dangerous life, working instead as an honest, impoverished housekeeper, her sister's card skills had become rusty. How else to explain the fact that, instead of winning, Bree had lost everything to her hated ex-boyfriend with the turn of a single card?

Vladimir Xendzov had separated the sisters, forcibly sending Josie back to the mainland on his private jet. She'd spent her last paycheck to fly back, desperate to get Bree out of his clutches. For forty-four hours now, since the dreadful night of the game, Josie had only managed to hold it together because she knew that, should everything else fail, she had one guaranteed fallback plan.

But now she actually had to fall back on the plan, it felt like falling on a sword.

Josie looked up again at the top of the skyscraper. The windows of the penthouse gleamed red, like fire, above the low-hanging clouds of Honolulu.

She'd caused her sister to lose her freedom. She would save her—by selling herself in marriage to Vladimir Xendzov's greatest enemy.

His younger brother.

The enemy of my enemy is my friend, she repeated to herself. And, considering the way the Xendzov brothers had tried to destroy each other for the past ten years, Kasimir Xendzov must be her new best friend. Right?

A lump rose in her throat.

I would marry the devil himself...

Slowly, Josie forced her feet off the sidewalk. Her legs wobbled as she crossed the street. She dodged a passing tour bus, flinching as it honked angrily.

There was no backing out now.

"Can I help you?" the doorman said inside the lobby, eyeing her messy ponytail, wrinkled T-shirt and cheap flip-flops.

Josie licked her dry lips. "I'm here to get married. To one of your residents."

He didn't bother to conceal his incredulity. "*You?* Are going to marry someone who lives *here?*"

She nodded. "Kasimir Xendzov."

His jaw dropped. "You mean His *Highness?* The *prince?*" he spluttered, gesticulating wildly. "Get out of here before I call the police!"

"Look, please just call him, all right? Tell him Josie Dalton is here and I've changed my mind. My answer is now yes."

"*Call* him? I'll do nothing of the sort." The doorman pinched his nose with his thumb and finger. "You must be delusional...if you think you can just walk in off the street..."

Josie rummaged through her backpack.

"His Highness's presence here is secret. He is here on *vacation*..."

"See?" she said desperately, holding out a business card. "He gave me this three days ago. When he proposed to me. At a salad bar near Waikiki."

"Salad bar," the doorman snorted. "As if the prince would ever..." He saw the embossed seal, and snatched the card from her hand. Turning over the card, he read the hard masculine scrawl on the back: *For when you change your mind.* "But you're not his type," he said faintly.

"I know," Josie sighed. Twenty pounds overweight, frumpy and unstylish, she was painfully aware that she was no man's type. Fortunately Kasimir Xendzov wished to marry her for reasons that had nothing to do with love—or even lust. "Just call him, will you?"

The man reached for the phone on his desk. He dialed. Turning away, he spoke in a low voice. A few moments later, he faced Josie with an utterly bewildered expression.

"His bodyguard says you're to go straight up," he said in shock. He pointed his finger towards an elevator. "Thirty-ninth floor. And, um, congratulations, miss."

"Thank you," Josie murmured, tugging her knapsack higher on her shoulder as she turned away. She felt the doorman watching her as she crossed the elegant lobby, her flip-flops echoing against the marble floor. She numbly got on the elevator. On the thirty-ninth floor, the door opened with a ding. Cautiously, she crept out into a hallway.

"Welcome, Miss Dalton." Two large, grim-looking bodyguards were waiting for her. In a quick, professional motion, one of them frisked her as the other one rifled through her bag.

"What are you checking for?" Josie said with an awkward laugh. "You think I would bring a hand grenade? To a wedding proposal?"

The bodyguards did not return her smile. "She's clear," one of them said, and handed her back the knapsack. "Please go in, Miss Dalton."

"Um. Thanks." Looking at the imposing door, she clutched her bag against her chest. "He's in there?"

He nodded sternly. "His Highness is expecting you."

Josie swallowed hard. "Right. I mean, great. I mean…" She turned back to them. "He's a good guy, right? A good employer? He can be trusted?"

The bodyguards stared back at her, their faces impassive.

"His Highness is expecting you," the first one repeated in an expressionless voice. "Please go in."

"Okay." *You robot,* she added silently, irritated.

Whatever. She didn't need reassurance. She'd just listen to her intuition. To her heart.

Which meant Josie was *really* in trouble. There was a reason her dying father had left her a large parcel of Alaskan land in an unbreakable trust, which she could not receive until she was either twenty-five—three years from now—or married. Even when she was a child, Black Jack Dalton had known his naive, trusting younger daughter needed all the help she could get. To say she could be naive about people was an understatement.

But it's a good quality, Bree had told her sadly two days ago. *I wish I had more of it.*

Bree. Josie could only imagine what her older sister was going through right now, as a prisoner of that other billionaire tycoon, Kasimir Xendzov's brother. Closing her eyes, she took a deep breath.

"For Bree," she whispered, and flung open the penthouse door.

The lavish foyer was empty. Stepping nervously across the marble floor, hearing the echo of her steps, she looked up at a soaring chandelier illuminating the sweeping staircase. This penthouse was like a mansion in the sky, she thought in awe.

Josie's lips parted when she saw the view through the floor-to-ceiling windows. Crossing the foyer to the great room, she looked out at the twinkling lights of the still-dark city, and beyond that, pink and orange sunrise sparkling across the Pacific Ocean.

"So…you changed your mind."

His low, masculine purr came from behind her.

She stiffened then, bracing herself, slowly turned around.

Prince Kasimir Xendzov's incredible good looks still hit her like a fierce blow. He was even more impossibly handsome than she remembered. He was tall, around six foot three, with broad shoulders and a hard-muscled body. His blue eyes were electric against tanned skin and dark hair. The expensive cut of his dark suit and tie, and the gleaming leather of his black shoes spoke of money—while the ruthlessness in his eyes and chiseled jawline screamed *power*.

In spite of her efforts, Josie was briefly thunderstruck.

Normally, she had no problems talking to people. As far as she was concerned, there was no such thing as a stranger. But Kasimir left her tongue-tied. No man this handsome had ever paid her the slightest notice. In fact, she wasn't sure there *was* any other man on earth with Kasimir's breathtaking masculine beauty. Looking into his darkly handsome face, she almost forgot to breathe.

"The last time I saw you, you said you'd never marry me." Kasimir slowly looked her over, from her flip-flops to her jeans and T-shirt. "For *any* price."

Josie's cheeks turned pink. "Maybe I was a bit hasty," she stammered.

"You threw your drink in my face."

"It was an accident!" she protested.

He lifted an incredulous dark eyebrow. "You jumped up and ran out of the restaurant."

"You just surprised me!" Three nights ago, on Christmas Eve, Kasimir had called her at the Hale Ka'nani Hotel, where she was working as a house-keeper. "My sister told me to never talk to you," she'd blurted out when he introduced himself. "I'm hanging up."

"Then you'll miss the best offer of your life," he'd replied silkily. He'd asked her to meet him at a hole-in-the-wall restaurant near Waikiki Beach. In spite of knowing he was forbidden—or perhaps because of it—she was intrigued by his mysterious proposal. And then she'd been even more shocked to find out he'd meant a real proposal. *Marriage.*

"You ran away from me," Kasimir said quietly, taking a step towards her, "as if you were being chased by the devil himself."

She swallowed.

"Because I did think you were the devil," she whispered.

His blue eyes narrowed in disbelief. "This is your way of saying you'll marry me?"

She shook her head. "You don't understand," she choked out. "You…"

Her throat closed. How could she explain that even though he and his brother had ruined their lives ten years ago, she'd still been electrified by Kasimir's bright blue eyes when he'd asked her to marry him? How to explain that, even though she knew it was only to get his hands on her land, she'd been overwhelmed by too many years of yearning for some man, any man, to notice her—and that she'd been tempted to blurt out *Yes,* betraying all her ideals about love and marriage?

How could she possibly explain such pathetic, naive stupidity? She couldn't.

"Why did you change your mind?" he asked in a low voice. "Do you need the money?"

They did need to pay off the dangerous men who'd pursued them for ten years, demanding payment of their dead father's long-ago debts. But Josie shook her head.

"Then is it the title of princess that you want?"

Josie threw him a startled glance. "Really?"

"Many women dream of it."

"Not me." She shook her head with a snort. "Besides, my sister told me your title's worthless. You might be the grandson of a Russian prince, but it's not like you actually own any land—"

Whoops. She cut off in midsentence at his glare.

"We once owned hundreds of thousands of acres in Russia," he said coldly. "And we owned the homestead in Alaska for nearly a hundred years, since my great-grandmother fled Siberia. It is rightfully ours."

"Sorry, but your brother sold your homestead to my father fair and square!"

He took a step towards her.

"Against my will," he said softly. "Without my knowledge."

Josie took an unwilling step back from the icy glitter in his blue eyes. A self-made billionaire, Kasimir Xendzov was known to be a ruthless, heartless playboy whose main interest, even more than dating supermodels or adding to his pile of money, was destroying his older brother, who had cheated him out of their business partnership right before it would have made him hundreds of millions of dollars.

"Are you afraid of me?" he asked suddenly.

"No," she lied, "why would I be?"

"There are...rumors about me. That I am more than ruthless. That I am—" he tilted his head, his blue eyes bright "—half-insane, driven mad by my hunger for revenge."

Her mouth went dry. "It's not true." She gulped, then said weakly, "Um, is it?"

He gave a low, threatening laugh. "If it were, I would hardly admit it." He turned away, pacing a step before he looked back at her. "So you've changed your mind. But has it occurred to you," he said softly, "that I might have changed my mind about marrying *you?*"

Josie looked up with an intake of breath. "You— wouldn't!"

He shrugged. "Your rejection of me three days ago was definitive."

Fear, real fear, rushed through Josie's heart. She'd

gambled her last money to come here. Without Kasimir's help, Bree would be lost. She'd be Vladimir Xendzov's possession. His *slave*. Forever. Her shoulders felt tight as hot tears rushed behind her eyes. Desperately, she grabbed his arm.

"No—please! You said you'd do anything to get the land back. You said you made a promise to your dying father. You—" She frowned, suddenly distracted by the hard muscle of his biceps. "Jeez, how much weight lifting do you do?"

He looked at her. Blushing, she dropped his arm. She took a deep breath.

"Just tell me. Do you still want to marry me?"

Kasimir's handsome face was impassive. "I need to understand your reason. If it's not to be a princess…"

She gave a choked laugh. "As if I'd marry someone for a worthless title!"

His dark eyebrow lifted. "For your information, my title isn't worthless. It's an asset. You'd be surprised how many people are impressed by it."

"You mean you use it as a shameless marketing tool for your business interests."

His lips curved with amusement. "So you do understand."

"I hope you're not expecting me to bow."

"I don't want you to bow." He looked up, his blue eyes intent. "I just want you to marry me. Right now. Today."

Staring at his gorgeous face, Josie's heart stopped. "So you do still want to marry me?"

He gave her a slow-rising smile that made his eyes crinkle. "Of course I want to marry you. It's all I've wanted."

He was looking down at her…as if he cared.

Of course he cares, she told herself savagely. *He cares about getting his family's land back. That's it.*

But when he looked at her like that, it was too easy to forget that. Her heart pounded. She felt… desired.

Josie tried to convince herself she didn't feel it. She didn't feel a strange tangle of tension and breathless need. She *didn't.*

Kasimir reached out a hand to touch her cheek. "But tell me what changed your mind."

The warm sensuality of his fingers against her skin made her tremble. No man had touched her so intimately. His fingertips were calloused—clearly he was accustomed to hard work—but they were tapered, sensitive fingers of a poet.

But Prince Kasimir Xendzov was no poet. Trembling, she looked down at his strong wrist, at his tanned, thick forearm laced with dark hair. He was a fighter. A warrior. He could crush her with one hand.

"Josie."

"My sister," she whispered, then stopped, her throat dry.

"Bree changed your mind?" Dropping his hand, he walked around her. "I find that hard to believe."

She took a deep breath.

"Your brother kidnapped her," she choked out. "I want you to save her."

She waited for him to express shock, elation, rage, *something*. But his expression didn't change.

"You…" He frowned, narrowing his eyes. "Wait. Vladimir *kidnapped* her?"

She bit her lip, then her shoulders slumped. "Well, I guess technically," she said in a small voice, "you could say she wagered herself to him in a card game. And lost."

His lip curled. "It was a lovers' game. No woman would wager herself otherwise." His eyes narrowed. "My brother always had a weakness for her. After ten years apart, they're no doubt deliriously happy they've made up their quarrel."

"Are you crazy?" she cried. "Bree hates him!"

"What!"

Josie shook her head. "He *forced* her to go with him."

His handsome face suddenly looked cheerful. "I see."

"And it's all my fault." A lump rose in her throat, and she covered her eyes. "The night after you proposed, my boss invited me to join a private poker game. I hoped I could win enough to pay off my father's old debts, and I snuck out while Bree was sleeping." She swallowed. "She never would have let me go. She forbade me ever to gamble, plus she didn't trust Mr. Hudson."

"Why?"

"I think it was mostly the way he hired us from Seattle, sight unseen, with one-way plane tickets to Hawaii. At the time, we were both too desperate to care, but…" She sighed. "She was right. There was something kind of…weird about it. But I didn't listen." She lifted her tearful gaze to his. "Bree lost everything on the turn of a single card. Because of me."

He looked down at her, his expression unreadable. "And you think *I* can save her."

"I know you can. You're the only one powerful enough to stand up to him. The only one on earth willing to battle with Vladimir Xendzov. Because you hate him the most." She took a deep breath. "Please," she whispered. "You can take my land. I don't care. But if you don't save Bree, I don't know how I'll live with myself."

Kasimir stared at her for a long moment.

"Here." He reached for the heavy backpack on her shoulder. "Let me take that."

"You don't need to—"

"You're swaying on your feet," he said softly. "You look as if you haven't slept in days. No wonder. Flying to Seattle and back…"

Without her bag weighing her down, she felt so light she almost felt dizzy. "I told you I went to Seattle?"

He froze, then relaxed as he looked back at her. "Of course you did," he said smoothly. "How else would I know?"

Yes, indeed, how would he? After almost no sleep for two days, she was starting to get confused. Rubbing her cheek with her shoulder, she confessed, "I am a little tired. And thirsty."

"Come with me. I'll get you a drink."

"Why are you being nice to me?" she blurted out, not moving.

He frowned. "Why wouldn't I be nice to you?"

"It always seems that the more handsome a man is, the more of a jerk he is. And you are very, very..."

Their eyes locked, and her throat cut off. Her cheeks burned as she muttered, "Never mind."

He gave her a crooked grin. "Whatever your sister might have told you about me, I'm not the devil. But I am being remiss in my manners. Let's get you that drink."

Carrying her backpack over his shoulder, he turned down the hallway. Josie watched him go, her eyes tracing the muscular shape of his back beneath his jacket and chiseled rear end.

Then she shook her head, irritated with herself. Why did she have to blurt out every single thought in her head? Why couldn't she just show discipline and quiet restraint, like Bree? Why did she have to be such a goofball all the time, the kind of girl who'd start conversations with random strangers on any topic from orchids to cookie recipes, then give them her bus money?

This time wasn't my fault, she thought mutinously, following him down the hall. He was far too handsome. No woman could possibly manage sensible thinking beneath the laser-like focus of those blue eyes!

Kasimir led her to a high-ceilinged room lined with leather-bound books on one side, and floor-to-ceiling windows with a view of the city on the other. Tossing her backpack on a long table of polished inlaid wood, he walked over to the wet bar on the other side of the library. "What will you have?"

"Tap water, please," she said faintly.

He frowned back at her. "I have sparkling mineral water. Or I could order coffee…"

"Just water. With ice, if you want to be fancy."

He returned with a glass.

"Thanks," she said. She glugged down the icy, delicious water.

He watched her. "You're an unusual girl, Josie Dalton."

Unusual didn't sound good. She wiped her mouth. "I am?" she echoed uncertainly, lowering the glass.

"It's refreshing to be with a woman who makes absolutely no effort to impress me."

She snorted. "Trying to impress you would be a waste of time. I know a man like you would never be interested in a girl like me—not *genuinely* interested," she mumbled.

He looked down at her, his blue eyes breath-taking.

"You're selling yourself short," he said softly, and Josie felt it again—that strange flash of heat.

She swallowed. "You're being nice, but I know there's no point in pretending to be something I'm not." She sighed. "Even if I sometimes wish I could."

"Unusual. And honest." Turning, he went to the wet bar and poured himself a short glass of amber-colored liquid. He returned, then took a slow, thoughtful sip.

"All right. I'll get your sister back for you," he said abruptly.

"You will!" If there was something strange about his tone, Josie was too weak with relief to notice. "When?"

"After we're wed. Our marriage will last until the land in Alaska is legally transferred to me." He looked straight into her eyes. "And I'll bring her to you, and set you both free. Is that what you want?"

Isn't that what she'd just said? "Yes," she cried.

Setting down his drink on the polished wooden table, he held out his hand. "Deal."

Slowly, she reached out her hand. She felt the hot, calloused hollow of his palm, felt his strong fingers interlace with hers. A tremble raced through her. Swallowing, she lifted her gaze to his handsome face, to those electric-blue eyes, and it was like staring straight at the sun.

"I hope it won't be too painful for you," she stammered, "being married to me."

His hand tightened over hers. "As you'll be my only wife, ever," he said softly, "I think I'll enjoy you a great deal."

"Your only wife *ever?*" Her brow furrowed. "That seems a little pessimistic of you. I mean—" she licked her lips awkwardly "—I'm sure you'll meet someone someday..."

Kasimir gave a low, humorless laugh.

"Josie, my sweet innocent one—" he looked at her with a smile that didn't reach his eyes "—you are the answer to my every prayer."

Prince Kasimir Xendzov hadn't started the feud ten years ago with his brother.

As a child, he'd idolized Vladimir. He'd been proud of his older brother, of his loving parents, of his family, of his home. Their great-grandfather had been one of the last great princes of Russia, before he'd died fighting for the White Army in Siberia, after sending his beloved wife and baby son to safety in Alaskan exile. Since then, for four generations, the Xendzovs had lived in self-sufficient poverty on an Alaskan homestead far from civilization. To Kasimir, it had been an enchanted winter kingdom.

But his older brother had hated the isolation and uncertainty—growing their own vegetables, canning them for winter, hunting rabbits for meat. He'd hated the lack of electricity and indoor plumbing. As Kasimir had played, battling with sticks as swords and jousting against the pine trees, Vladimir had buried his nose in business books and impatiently waited for their twice-a-year visits to Fairbanks. "Someday, I'll have a better life," he'd vowed, cursing as he scraped ice off the inside window of their shared room. "I'll buy clothes instead of making them. I'll drive a Ferrari. I'll fly around the world and eat at fine restaurants."

Kasimir, two years younger, had listened breathlessly. "Really, Volodya?" But though he'd idolized his older brother, he hadn't understood Vladimir's restlessness. Kasimir loved their home. He liked going hunting with their father and listening to him read books in Russian by the wood-burning stove at night. He liked chopping wood for their mother, feeling the roughness of an ax handle in his hand, and having the satisfaction of seeing the pile of wood climb steadily against the side of the log cabin. To him, the wild Alaskan forest wasn't isolating. It was freeing.

Home. Family. Loyalty. Those were the things Kasimir cared about.

Right after their father died unexpectedly, Vladimir got news he'd been accepted to the best mining college in St. Petersburg, Russia. Their widowed mother had wept with joy, for it had been their father's dream. But with no money for tuition, Vladimir had put off school and gone to work at a northern mine to save money.

Two years later, Kasimir had applied to the same college for one reason: he felt someone had to watch his brother's back. He didn't expect that he'd have the money to leave Alaska for many years, so he'd been surprised tuition money for them both was suddenly found.

It was only later he'd discovered Vladimir had convinced their mother to sell their family's last precious asset, a jeweled necklace hundreds of years old that had once belonged to their great-grandmother, to a collector.

He'd felt betrayed, but he'd tried to forgive. He'd told himself that Vladimir had done it for their good.

Right after college, Kasimir had wanted to return to Alaska to take care of their mother, who'd become ill. Vladimir convinced him that they should start their own business instead, a mining business. "It's the only way we'll be sure to always have money to take care of her." Instead, when the banks wouldn't loan them enough money, Vladimir had convinced their mother to sell the six hundred and thirty-eight acres that had been in the Xendzov family for four generations—ever since Princess Xenia Petrovna Xendzova had arrived on Alaskan shores as a heartbroken exile, with a baby in her arms.

Kasimir had been furious. For the first time, he'd yelled at his brother. How could Vladimir have done such a thing behind his back, when he knew Kasimir had made a fervent deathbed promise to their father never to sell their land for any reason?

"Don't be selfish," Vladimir said coldly. "You think Mom could do all the work of the homestead without us?" And the money had in part paid for their mother to spend her last days at a hospice in Fairbanks. Kasimir's heart still twisted when he thought of it. His eyes narrowed.

The real reason they'd lost their home had been Vladimir's need to secure the most promising mining rights. What mattered: a younger brother's honor, a mother's home, or his need to establish their business with good cash flow and the best equipment?

"Don't worry," his brother had told him carelessly. "Once we're rich, you can easily buy it back again."

Kasimir set his jaw. He should have cut off all ties with his brother then and there. Instead, after their mother died, he'd felt more bound than ever to his brother—his only family. They strove for a year to build their business partnership, working eighteen-hour days in harsh winter conditions. Kasimir had been certain they'd soon earn their first big payout, and buy their home back again.

He hadn't known that Black Jack Dalton, the land's buyer, had put the land in an irrevocable trust for his child. Or that, as recompense for Kasimir's loyalty, hard work and honesty, at the end of that year Vladimir would cut him out of the partnership and cheat him out of his share of half a billion dollars.

Now, even though Kasimir had long since built up his own billion-dollar mining company, his body still felt tight with rage whenever he remembered how the brother he'd adored had stabbed him in the back. Even once Kasimir regained the land, he knew it would never feel like home. Because he'd never be that same loyal, loving, idealistic, stupid boy again.

No. Kasimir hadn't started the feud with his brother.

But he would end it.

"I'm the answer to your prayer?" a sweet, feminine voice said, sounding puzzled. "How?"

Kasimir's eyes focused on Josie Dalton, standing in front of him in the library of his Honolulu penthouse.

Her brown eyes were large and luminous, fringed with long black lashes—but he saw the weary gray shadows beneath. Her skin was smooth and creamy—but pale, and smudged on one cheek with dust. Her mouth was full and pink—but the lower lip was chapped, as if she'd spent the last two days chewing on it in worry. Her light brown hair, which he could imagine thick and lustrous tumbling down her shoulders, was half pulled up in a disheveled ponytail.

Josie Dalton was not beautiful—no. But she was attractive in her own way, all youth and dewy innocence and overblown curves. He cut off the thought. He did not intend to let himself explore further.

He cleared his throat. "I've wanted our land back for a long time." His voice was low and gravelly, even to his own ears. "I'll make the arrangements for our wedding at once."

"What kind of arrangements?" She bit her lip anxiously, her soft brown eyes wide. "You don't mean a—a honeymoon?"

He looked at her sharply. She blushed. Her pink cheeks looked very charming. Who blushed anymore? "No. I don't mean a honeymoon."

"Good." Her cheeks burned red as she licked her lips. "I'm glad. I mean, I know this is a marriage in name only," she said hastily, holding up her hand. "And that's the only reason I could agree to..."

Her voice trailed off. Looking down, he caught her staring at his lips.

She was so unguarded, so innocent, he thought in wonder. Soft, pretty. Virginal. It would be very easy to seduce her.

Fortunately, she wasn't his type. His typical mistress was sleek and sophisticated. She lavished hours at the salon and the gym as though it was her full-time job. Véronique, in Paris. Farah, in Cairo. Oksana, in Moscow. Exotic women who knew how to seduce a man, who kept their lips red and their eyes lined with kohl, who greeted him at the door in silk lingerie and always had his favorite vodka chilled in the freezer. They welcomed him quickly into bed and spoke little, and even then, they never quite said what they meant. They were easy to slide into bed with.

And more importantly: they were very easy to leave.

Josie Dalton, on the other hand, expressed every thought—and if she forgot to say anything with words, her face said it anyway. She wore no makeup and clearly saw her hair as a chore, rather than an asset. In that baggy T-shirt and jeans, she obviously had no interest in fashion, or even in showing her figure to its best effect.

But Kasimir was glad she wasn't trying to lure him. Because he had no intention of seducing her. It would only complicate things that didn't need to be complicated. And it would hurt a tenderhearted young woman whom he didn't want to hurt—at least not more than he had to.

No. He was going to treat Josie Dalton like gold.

"So what other…arrangements…are you talking about?" she said haltingly. She lifted her chin, her eyes suddenly sparkling. "Maybe a wedding cake?"

This time, he really did laugh. "You want a cake?"

"I do love a good wedding cake, with butter-cream-frosting roses…" she said wistfully.

"Your wish is my command, my lady," he said gravely.

Her expression drooped, and she shook her head with a sigh. "But I'd better not."

He rolled his eyes. "Don't tell me you're on a diet."

"Do I look like I watch my weight?" she snapped, then flushed guiltily. "Sorry. I'm a little grumpy. My flight ran out of meals before they reached my aisle, and I haven't eaten for twelve hours. I would have bought something at the airport but I only have three dollars and thought maybe I should save it."

Her voice trailed off. Kasimir had already turned away, crossing to the desk. He pressed the intercom button.

"Sir?"

"Send up a breakfast plate."

"Two, Your Highness?"

"Just one. But make it full and make it quick." He glanced back at Josie. "Anything special you'd like to eat, Miss Dalton?"

She gaped back at him, her mouth open.

He turned back to the intercom and said smoothly, "Just send everything you've got."

"Of course, sir."

Taking her unresisting hand, Kasimir led her to the soft blue sofa and sat beside her. She stared at him, apparently mesmerized, as if he'd done something truly shocking by simply ordering her some breakfast when she said she was hungry.

"You were saying," he prompted.

"I was?"

"Wedding cake. Why you don't want it."

"Right." Ripping her hand away nervously, she

squared her shoulders and said in a firm voice, "This is just a business arrangement, so there's no point to wedding cake. Or a wedding dress. I think it's best for both of us—" she looked at him sideways, not quite meeting his eyes "—to keep our marriage on a strictly professional basis."

"As you wish." He lifted an eyebrow. "You are the bride. You are the boss."

She swallowed, turning her head to look at him nervously. "I am?"

He smiled. "I know that much about how a wedding works."

"Oh." Josie's face was the color of roses and cream as she chewed on her full, pink bottom lip. "You're being very, um—" her voice faltered and seemed to stumble "—nice to me."

Kasimir's smile twisted. "Will you stop saying that."

"But it's true."

"I'm being strictly professional, just as you said. Courtesy is part of business."

"Oh." She considered this, then slowly nodded. "In that case..."

"I'm glad you agree." He wondered if she would still accuse him of kindness if she knew the truth about what he intended to do with her. Or exactly why she was the answer to his prayer.

An hour ago, he'd been on the phone in his home office, barely listening to his VP of acquisitions drone on about how they could sabotage Vladimir's imminent takeover of Arctic Oil. He'd been too busy thinking about how his own recent plan to embarrass his brother had blown up in his face.

Kasimir had long despised Bree Dalton, the con artist he blamed for the first rift between the brothers ten years ago. All this time, he'd kept track of her from a distance, waiting for her to go back to her old ways (she hadn't) or to agree to let Josie marry him to get the land (she wouldn't, and he could go to hell for asking).

Kasimir had finally decided to try another way: Josie herself.

Until they'd met at the Salad Shack a few days ago, all he'd known of Josie was in a file from a private investigator, with a grainy photograph. Six months ago in Seattle, the man had tested her by dropping a wallet full of cash in the aisle of a grocery store in front of her. Josie had run two blocks after the man's car, catching up with him at a stoplight, to breathlessly give the wallet back, untouched. "Girl's so honest, she's a nut," the investigator had grumbled.

So finally, Kasimir had come to a decision. Knowing his brother was recuperating from a recent car-racing injury in Oahu with a private weekly poker game at the Hale Ka'nani, he'd bribed the general manager of the resort, Greg Hudson, to hire the Dalton sisters as housekeepers. He'd hoped Vladimir would have a run-in with Bree Dalton, causing him a humiliating scene, but that was just an amusement. Kasimir's real goal in coming here had been to try to negotiate for the land, and the requisite marriage, directly with Josie Dalton.

He shouldn't have been surprised that she'd flung her soda at him and run out. Or that, according to the report he'd gotten from Greg Hudson, not only had there been no screaming match between Vladimir and Bree, they'd apparently fallen into each other's arms at the poker game. Bree had won back the entire amount of her sister's wager, then promptly accepted Vladimir's offer to a single-card draw between them—a million dollars versus possession of Bree.

Reintroducing the formerly engaged couple to happiness after ten years of estrangement, had never been Kasimir's plan. For the past day and a half, he'd been grinding his teeth in fury. He'd spent last night dancing at a club, women hitting on him right and left, until even that started to irritate him, and he'd gone home early—and alone.

Then, like a miracle, he'd been woken from sleep with the news that Josie Dalton was here and wished to marry him after all.

And now, here she was. He had her. She'd just changed his whole world—forever.

He could have kissed her.

"I will be happy to get you a cake," he said fervently. "And a designer wedding gown, and a ten-carat diamond ring." Reaching for her hand, he kissed it, then looked into her eyes. "Just tell me what you want, and it's yours."

Her cheeks turned a darker shade of pink. He felt her hand tremble in his own before she yanked it away. "Just bring my sister home. Safely away from your brother."

"You have my word. Soon." He rose to his feet. "I must call my lawyer. In the meantime, please take some time to rest." He gestured to the bookshelves of first-edition books. "Read, if you like. Your breakfast will be here at any moment." He gave a slight bow. "Please excuse me."

"Kasimir?"

He froze. Had Josie somehow guessed his plans? Was it possible her expressive brown eyes had seen right through his twisted, heartless soul? Hands clenched at his sides, body taut, Kasimir turned back to face her.

Josie's eyes were shining, her expression bright as a new penny, as she leaned back against the sofa pillows. His gaze traced unwillingly over the patterns on her skin, along the curve of her full breasts beneath her T-shirt, left by the soft morning light.

"Thank you for saving my sister," she whispered. She took a deep breath. "And me."

Uneasiness went through him, but he shook it away from his well-armored soul. He gave her a stiff nod. "We will both benefit from this arrangement. Both of us," he repeated stonily, squashing his conscience like a newly sprouted weed.

"But I'll never forget it," she said softly, looking at him with gratitude that approached hero-worship. Her brown eyes glowed, and she was far more beautiful than he'd first realized. "I don't care what people say. You're a good man."

His jaw tightened. Without a word, he turned away from her. Once he reached his home office, he phoned his chief lawyer to arrange the prenuptial agreement and discuss ways to break Josie's trust as quickly as possible. The discussion took longer than expected. When Kasimir returned to the library an hour later, he found Josie curled up fast asleep on the sofa, with a cold, untouched breakfast tray on the table beside her.

Kasimir looked down at her. She looked so young, sleeping. Had he ever been that young? She couldn't be more than twenty-two, eleven years younger than he was, and more stupidly innocent than he'd been at that age. In spite of himself, he felt an unwelcome desire to take care of her. To protect her.

His jaw set. And so he would. For as long as she was his prisoner—that was to say, his wife.

He reached a hand out to wake her, then stopped. He looked down at the gray shadows beneath her eyes. No. Let her sleep. Their wedding could wait a few hours. She deserved a place to rest, a safe harbor. And so he would be for her....

Carefully, he picked her up into his arms, cradling her against his chest. He carried her upstairs to the guest room. Without turning on the light, he set her gently on the mattress, beside the blue silk pillows. He stepped back, looking down at her in the shadowy room.

He heard her sweetly wistful voice. *I do love a good wedding cake with buttercream-frosting roses.*

Kasimir had told her the truth. She would be his only wife. He never intended to have a real marriage. Or trust any human soul enough to give them the ability to stab him in the back. This would be as close as he'd ever get to holy matrimony. For the few brief weeks of the marriage, Josie Dalton would be the closest he'd ever have to a wife. *To a family.*

He took a deep breath. She'd make an exceptional wife for any man. She was an old-fashioned kind of woman, the kind they didn't make anymore. From his investigator's reports, he knew Josie was ridiculously honest and scrupulously kind. Six months ago, a different private investigator had her under surveillance in Seattle. He'd dressed as a homeless street person, which should have rendered him invisible. Not to Josie, though. "She came right up to me to ask if I was all right," the man reported in amazement, "or if I needed anything. Then she insisted on giving me her brown-bag lunch." He'd smiled. "Peanut butter and jelly!"

What kind of girl did that? Who had a heart that unjaded and, well—soft?

Unlike Vladimir and Bree, unlike Kasimir himself, Josie deserved to be protected. She was an innocent. She'd done nothing to earn the well-deserved revenge he planned for the other two.

Even though it would still hurt her.

He felt another spasm beneath his solar plexus.

Guilt, he realized in shock. He hadn't felt that emotion for a long time. He wouldn't let it stop him. But he'd be as gentle as he could to her.

Turning away from Josie's sleeping form, he went back downstairs to his home office. He phoned his head secretary, and ten minutes later, he was contacted by Honolulu's top wedding planner. Afterward, he tossed his phone onto his desk.

Swiveling his chair, he looked out the window overlooking the penthouse's rooftop pool. Bright sunlight glimmered over the blue water, and beyond that, he could see the city and the distant ocean melting into the blue sky.

For ten years, he'd been wearing Vladimir down, fighting his company tooth and claw with his own, getting his attention the only way he knew how—by making him pay with tiny stings, death by a thousand cuts.

But getting Bree Dalton to betray Vladimir would be the deepest cut of all. The fatal one.

Rising to his feet, Kasimir stood in front of the window, hands tucked behind his back as he gazed out unseeingly towards the Pacific. He'd give his lawyer a few weeks to transfer possession of Josie's land back to his control. By then, once the two little lovebirds were enmeshed in each other, Kasimir would blackmail Bree into stealing his brother's company away.

He narrowed his eyes. Bree would crush Vladimir's heart beneath her boot, and his brother would finally know what it felt like to have someone else change his life, against his will, when Bree betrayed him.

She'd have no choice. Kasimir had all the ammunition he needed to make Bree Dalton do exactly as he wanted. A cold smile crossed his lips.

He had her sister.

CHAPTER TWO

JOSIE'S EYELIDS FLUTTERED, then flew open as she sat up with a sharp intake of breath.

She was still fully dressed. She'd been sleeping on an enormous bed, in a strange bedroom. The masculine, dark-floored bedroom was flooded with golden light from the windows.

How long had she been sleeping? She yawned, and her mouth felt dry, as if it was lined with cotton. Who had brought her here? Could it have been Kasimir himself?

The thought of being carried in those strong arms, against his powerful chest, as she slept on unaware, caused her to tremble. She looked down at the mussed white bedspread.

Could it possibly be his bed…?

With a gulp, Josie jumped up as if it had burned her. The clock on the fireplace mantel said three o'clock. Gracious! She'd slept for hours. She stretched her arms above her head with another yawn. It had been nice of Kasimir to let her sleep. She felt so much better.

Until she saw herself in the full-length mirror on the other side of the bedroom. Wait. Was that what she looked like? She took three steps towards it, then sucked in her breath in horror, covering her mouth with her hand.

Josie knew she wasn't the most fashionable dresser, and that she was a bit on the plump side, too. But she'd had no idea she looked *this* bad. She'd crossed the Pacific twice in the same rumpled T-shirt and wrinkled, oversize men's jeans that she'd bought secondhand last year. In her flight back from Seattle, she'd been crushed in the last row, in a sweaty middle seat between oversize businessmen who took her armrests and stretched their knees into her personal space. And she hadn't had a shower or even brushed her teeth for two days.

Josie gasped aloud, realizing she'd been grungy and gross like this when she'd been face-to-face with Kasimir. Picturing his sleek, expensive clothes, his perfect body, the way he looked so powerful and sexy as a Greek god with those amazing eyes and broad shoulders and chiseled cheekbones, her cheeks flamed.

She narrowed her eyes. She might be a frumpy nobody, but there was *no way* she was going to face him again, possibly on her fake wedding day, without a shower and some clean clothes. *No way!*

Looking around for her backpack, she saw it sitting by the door and snatched it up, then headed for the large en suite bathroom.

It was luxurious, all gleaming white marble and shining silver. Tossing her tattered backpack on the marble counter, where it looked extremely out of place, she started to dig through it for a toothbrush. Some great packing job, she thought in irritation. In the forty seconds she'd rushed around their tiny apartment in Honolulu, trying to flee before Vladimir Xendzov could collect Bree as his rightful property, Josie had grabbed almost nothing of use.

The top of a bikini—just the top, no bottom. Her mother's wool cardigan sweater, now frayed and darned. Some slippers. She hadn't even remembered to pack underwear. Gah!

Desperately, she dug further. A few cheap souvenirs from Waikiki. Her cell phone, now dead because she'd forgotten to pack the charger. A tattered Elizabeth Gaskell novel which had belonged to her mother when she was a high-school English teacher. A small vinyl photo album, that flopped open to a photo of her family taken a year before Josie was born.

Her heart twisted as she picked it up. In the picture, her mother was glowing with health, her father was beaming with pride and five-year-old Bree, with blond pigtails, had a huge toothless gap in her smile. Josie ran her hand over their faces. Beneath the clear plastic, the old photo was wrinkled at the edges from all the nights Josie had slept with it under her pillow as a child, while she was left alone with the babysitter for weeks at a time. Her parents and Bree looked so happy.

Before Josie was born.

It was an old grief, one she'd always lived with. If Josie had never been conceived, her mother wouldn't have put off chemotherapy treatments for the sake of her unborn child. Or died a month after Josie's birth, causing her father to go off the deep end, quitting his job as a math teacher and taking his seven-year-old poker-playing prodigy daughter Bree down the Alaskan coast to fleece tourists. Josie blinked back tears.

If she had never been born...

Her parents and Bree might still be happy and safe in a snug little suburban home.

Squaring her shoulders, she shook the thought away. Tucking the photo album back into her bag, she looked at her own bleak reflection, then grabbed her frayed toothbrush, drenched it in minty toothpaste and cleaned her teeth with a vengeance.

A moment later, she stepped into the steaming hot water of the huge marble shower. The rush of water felt good against her skin, like a massage against the tired muscles of her back and shoulders, washing all the dust and grime and grief away. Using some exotic orange-scented shampoo with Arabic writing—where on earth had Kasimir gotten that?—Josie washed her long brown hair thoroughly. Then she washed it again, just to be sure.

It was going to be all right, she repeated to herself. It would all be all right.

Soon, her sister would be safe.

Soon, her sister would be home.

And once Bree was free from Vladimir Xendzov's clutches, maybe Josie would finally have the guts to tell her what she felt in her heart, but had never been brave enough to say.

As much as she loved and appreciated all that Bree had sacrificed for her over the past ten years, Josie was no longer a child. She was twenty-two. She wanted to learn how to drive. To get a job on her own. To be allowed to go to bars, to date. She wanted the freedom to make mistakes, without Bree as an anxious mother hen, constantly standing over her shoulder.

She wanted to grow up.

Turning off the water, she got out of the shower. The large bathroom was steamy, the mirrors opaque with white fog. She wondered how long she'd been in the water. She didn't wear a watch because she hated to watch the passage of time, which seemed to go far too slowly when she was working, and rushed by at breakneck speed when she was not. Why, she'd often wondered, couldn't time rush by at work, and then slip into delicious slowness when she was at home, lasting and lasting, like sunlight on a summer's day?

Wrapping a plush white towel around her body, over skin that was scrubbed clean with orange soap and pink with heat, she looked at the sartorial choices offered by her backpack. Let's see. Which was better: a wool cardigan or a bikini top?

With a grumpy sigh, she looked back at the dirty, wrinkled T-shirt, jeans and white cotton panties and bra crumpled on the shining white tile of the bathroom floor. She'd worn those clothes for two days straight. The thought of putting them back over her clean skin was dreadful. But she had no other option.

Or did she…?

Her eyes fell upon something hanging on the back of the bathroom door that she hadn't noticed before. A white shift dress. Going towards it, she saw a note attached to the hanger.

Every bride needs a wedding dress. Join me at the rooftop pool when you're awake.

She smiled down at the hard black angles of his handwriting. She'd thought she hadn't wanted a dress, that she wanted to keep their wedding as dull and unromantic as possible. But now…how had he known the small gesture would mean so much?

Then she saw the dress's tag. Chanel. Holy cow. Maybe the gesture wasn't so small. For a moment, she was afraid to touch the fabric. Then she stroked the lace softly with her fingertips. It felt like a whisper. Like a dream.

Maybe everything really was going to be all right.

Josie exhaled, blinking back tears. She'd taken a huge gamble, using her last paycheck to come back to Honolulu, trusting Kasimir to help her. But it had paid off. For the first time in her life, she'd done something right.

It was a strangely intoxicating feeling.

Josie had always been the one who ruined things, not the one who saved them. She'd learned from a young age that the only way to make up for all the pain she'd caused everyone was just to take a book and go read quietly and invisibly in a corner, making as little trouble or fuss as possible.

But this time...

She tried to imagine her sister's face when Josie burst in with Prince Kasimir and saved her. Wouldn't Bree be surprised that her baby sister had done something important, something difficult, all by herself? *Josie,* her usually unflappable sister would blurt out, *how did you do this? You're such a genius!*

Josie smiled to herself, picturing the sweetness of that moment. Then she looked down at her naked body, pink with heat from the shower. Time to do her part, but maybe it wouldn't be so awful after all. How hard could it be, to get dressed in a fancy wedding gown, and marry a rich, handsome prince?

Pulling the white shift dress off the hanger, she stepped into it. Pulling it up her thighs, she gasped at the feel of the sensual fabric against her skin. It was a little short, though.

Josie frowned, looking down. It only reached to her mid-thigh. Maybe it would be all right, though. She reached back for the zipper. As long as it wasn't...

Tight. She stopped. The zipper wouldn't zip. Holding her breath, she sucked in her belly. Nervously, she moved the zipper up inch by inch, afraid she'd break it and ruin the expensive dress. Finally the zipper closed. She looked at herself in the mirror.

Her full breasts were pushed up by the tight dress, practically exploding out of the neckline. She looked way too grown-up and, well, *busty*. Bree would never have let her leave the house like this in a million years.

But it was either this or the dirty clothes. She decided she could live with tight. She'd just have to be careful not to bust a seam every time she moved.

Going to her backpack in mincing steps, she grabbed a brush and brushed her wet brown hair down her shoulders, leaving traces of dampness against the silk. She put on her pink flip-flops—it was either that or fuzzy slippers, and she was in Hawaii, after all—and some tinted lip balm. She left the bedroom with as much elegance as she could muster, her head held high.

Tottering down the stairs to the bottom floor of the penthouse, Josie went through the rooms until she finally found her way to the rooftop pool, with the help of the smiling housekeeper she'd found in the big kitchen. "That way, miss. Down the hall and through the salon."

The salon?

Josie went through a large room with a grand piano, then through the sliding door to the rooftop pool. She saw Kasimir at a large table, still dressed in his severely black suit, leaning back in his chair. He was talking on the phone, but when he saw her, his eyes widened.

Nervously, Josie walked along the edge of the pool towards him. She had to sway her hips unnaturally to move forward, and she felt a bead of sweat suddenly form between her breasts. The sun felt hot against her skin.

Or maybe it was just the way her bridegroom was looking at her.

"I'll talk to you later," he breathed to the person on the phone, never looking away from Josie, and he rose to his feet. His gaze seemed shocked as it traveled up and down her body. "What are you wearing?"

"The wedding dress. That you gave me. Should I have not?"

"That—" his voice sounded strangled "—is the dress I left you?"

"Yeah, um, it's a little tight," she said, her cheeks burning. She wasn't used to being the center of any man's attention, let alone a man like Prince Kasimir Xendzov. Then she bit her lip, afraid she'd sounded like she was complaining. "But it was really thoughtful of you to get me a wedding dress," she added quickly.

He slowly looked her up and down. "You look…"

She waited unhappily for his next word.

"…*fine,*" he finished huskily, and he pulled out a chair for her. "Please sit."

Fine? She exhaled. Fine. She could live with *fine.* "Thanks."

But could she sit down? Clutching the edges of the short hem, she sat down carefully. The expensive craftsmanship paid off. The seams held. She exhaled.

Until, looking down, she saw she was flashing way too much skin. With the dress tugged so hard downward, her breasts were thrust up even higher, and the fabric now just barely covered her nipples for decency. Trying to simultaneously pull the dress higher over her breasts and lower over her thighs, she bit her lip, glancing up in chagrin.

Fortunately, to her relief, as he sat down across the table from her, Kasimir's gaze seemed careful not to drop below her eyes. He indicated the lunch spread across the table. "You've come at the perfect time."

She looked at the chicken salad, fresh fruit and big rolls of crusty bread. It all looked delicious. But even Chanel craftsmanship would only go so far. "I probably shouldn't," she said glumly.

"Don't be ridiculous. You must be starving. You fell asleep before breakfast. You've not had a decent meal for days." Taking a plate, he started to load it with a bit of everything. "We can't have you fainting during our wedding this afternoon."

She almost laughed aloud. Her? Faint from hunger?

Food had always been Josie's guilty pleasure. She felt self-conscious about the extra pounds she carried around, sure, but not enough to give up the pastries and candy she loved. Unlike Bree, who boringly ate the same healthy salad and nuts and fish every day, Josie loved trying exotic new cuisine. Maybe she didn't have the money or courage to travel around the world, but eating at a Thai or Mexican or Indian restaurant was almost as good, wasn't it? Especially when she found a half-price coupon. She looked at the delicious meal in front of her. And this was even better than half price!

She gave him a sudden grin. "Who says there's no such thing as a free lunch, huh?"

"Glad you understand." Placing the full plate in front of her, Kasimir gave her a wicked grin. "You are going to be my wife, Josie. That means, as long as you are mine, all you will know—is pleasure."

Their eyes locked, and she felt that strange flutter in her belly—a flutter that had nothing to do with cookies, couscous or even chocolate. "Okay," she whispered as heat pulsed through her body. She unconsciously licked her lips. "If you insist."

"I'll admit the dress is a bit tight. Women's fashions are often a mystery to me," he said huskily. "I very rarely pay attention to them—except when I'm taking them off."

"I bet," she said shyly, shaking a little. Could he see that she was a virgin with zero sexual experience? Could he tell? Suddenly unable to meet his eyes, she dropped her own back to her plate. Even across the table, he felt so close to her. And too good-looking. Why did he have to be so good-looking? Not to mention sophisticated and powerful. He looked like a million bucks in that dark vested suit.

Sitting back in his chair, he filled himself a plate, then pushed a pile of papers towards her. "You need to sign this."

"What is it?"

"Our prenuptial agreement."

"Fantastic," she said, looking up in relief.

His eyebrows raised. "Not the usual reaction I'd expect."

"Remember, I want to keep our arrangement nice and official." She started reading through the first pages, pausing to sign and initial in places. As she read, she took a bite of a crusty bread, then a nibble of the ginger chicken salad. It was surprisingly good, with carrots, lettuce and cilantro. She ate some more. "Have you found my sister yet?"

"I might have an idea where Vladimir could have taken her."

"Where?"

"I'll look into it further." He tilted his head. "*After* we are married."

"Oh. Right. The deal." She took a deep breath. "But she's safe?"

He snorted. "What do you think?"

She looked up. "You think she is?"

"She is crafty. And sly. I doubt even my brother will be able to control her," he said dryly. "It's more likely she'd be putting him through hell."

Feeling reassured, she leaned her elbows against the table. "You don't like my sister, do you?"

"She's a liar," he said evenly. "A con artist."

"Not anymore!" Josie cried, stung.

"Ten years ago, she told my brother your land was legally hers to sell. Then she tried to distract him from doing his due diligence with her big weepy eyes and a low-cut blouse."

Josie licked her lips. "We were desperate. My father had just died, and violent men were demanding repayment of his debts—"

"Of course." He shrugged contemptuously. "Every criminal always has some hard-luck story. But our company was still new. We wanted our family's land back, but we could little afford to lose the thousands of dollars in earnest money she planned to steal from us. She had Vladimir so wrapped around her finger, she would have succeeded..."

She shook her head vehemently. "She told me the whole story. By then she'd already fallen in love with your brother, and was planning to throw herself on his mercy."

"On his mercy? Right. I told him the truth about

her, and he refused to believe me." He looked away. "I decided to fly back to our site in Russia, alone. At the airport, I drunkenly told a reporter the whole story. The next morning, when my brother found himself embarrassed in front of all the world, he pushed me out of our partnership. And out of a Siberian deal he signed two days later worth half a billion dollars."

"I'm sorry about the problems between you and your brother, but it wasn't Bree's fault!"

"No. It was Vladimir's. And mine." He narrowed his eyes. "But she still deserves to be punished."

"But she has been," Josie said, looking down unhappily at her empty plate. "She was going to tell your brother everything. To be honest, at any price. But he never gave her the chance. He deserted her without a word. And he left her to the wolves. Alone, and in charge of a twelve-year-old child." She lifted her gaze. "My sister has been punished. Believe me."

As he stared at her, his angry gaze slowly softened. "You alone are innocent in all this. I will bring her back to you. I swear it."

She gave an awkward laugh. "Stop it, will you? Stop being so—"

"You'd better not say *nice*," he threatened her.

She took a deep breath. "Just stop reminding me!"

"Of what?"

She spread her arms helplessly. "That you're a handsome, charming prince, and I—" She stopped.

"And you what?"

She blurted out, "I'm a total idiot who can't even remember to pack underwear!"

Oh, now she'd really done it. She wished she could clap a hand over her mouth, but it was too late. His eyes widened as he sucked in his breath.

"Are you telling me," he said in a low voice, "that right now, you're not wearing any underwear?"

Miserably, she shook her head, hating herself for blurting out every thought. Why, oh why, had she ever mentioned underwear? Why couldn't she keep her mouth shut?

His blue eyes moved slowly over her curves in the tight white dress. A muscle tightened in his jaw. "I see." He turned away, his jaw clenched. "We'll have to buy you some. After the wedding."

His voice was ice-cold. She'd offended him, she thought sadly. She buttered a delicious crusty roll, then slowly ate it as she tried to think of a way to change the subject. "Your Highness..."

He snorted. "I thought you said it was a worthless title."

"I changed my mind."

"Since when?"

She tried to grin. "Since I'm about to be a princess?"

"Just call me by my first name."

She hesitated... "Um, I'd rather not, actually. It just feels a little too personal right now. With you being so irritated..."

"I'm not irritated," he bit out.

"Your Highness…"

"Kasimir," he ordered.

She swallowed, looking away. But he waited. Taking a deep breath, she finally turned back to face him and whispered, "Kasimir."

Just his name on her lips felt very erotic, the *K* hard against her teeth, the *A* parting her lips, the *S* vibrating, sibilant against her skin as the *M-I-R* ended on her lips like a kiss.

He looked at her in the Hawaiian sunlight.

"Yes," he said softly. "Like that."

She swallowed, feeling out of her depth, drowning. "I like your name," she blurted out nervously. "It's an old Slavic name, isn't it? A warrior's name. 'Destroyer of the Peace.'" She was chattering, something she often did when she was nervous. "Very different from the meaning of your brother's…" *Uh-oh*. That topic wouldn't end well. She closed her mouth with a snap. "Sorry," she said weakly. "Never mind."

"Fascinating." His body was very still on the other side of the table, his voice cold again. "Go on. Tell me more."

She shrugged. "I've worked as a housekeeper for hotels for years, since I turned eighteen, and I listen to audio books from the library while I clean. It's amazing what you can learn," she mumbled. She gave him a bright smile. "Like about…um…botany, for instance. Did you know that there are only three types of orchid native to Hawaii? Everyone always thinks tons of orchids grow here in the rain forest, while the truth is that another place I once lived, Nevada, which is nothing but dry desert, has *twelve* different wild orchids in two distinct varieties. There was this, um, flower that…"

But Kasimir hadn't moved. He sat across from her beneath the hot Hawaiian sunshine, his arms folded as the water's reflection from the pool left patterns of light on his black suit. "You were telling me about the meaning of my brother's name."

She gulped. There was no help for it. "Vladimir. Well. Some people think it means 'He on the Side of Peace,' but most of the etymology seems to indicate the root *mir* is older still, from the Gothic, meaning 'Great in His Power.' And Vladimir is…" She hesitated.

Kasimir's eyes were hard now. She took a deep breath.

"'The Master of All,'" she whispered.

Hands clenched at his sides, Kasimir rose to his feet. Frightened by the fierce look in his eyes, she involuntarily shrank back in her chair. His hands abruptly relaxed.

"My brother is not all-powerful," he said simply. "And he will know it. Very soon."

"Wait." As he started to turn away, she jumped to her feet, grabbing his arm. "I'm sorry. I'm so stupid, always letting my mouth get ahead of my brain. My sister always says I need to be more careful."

"I'm not offended." Looking down at her, he gave her a smile that didn't quite meet his blue eyes. "You shouldn't listen to your sister. I respect a woman who speaks the truth without fear far more than one who uses silence to cover her lies."

"But I told you—she's not like that. Not anymore." With a weak laugh, she looked away. "If she were, we'd be rich right now, instead of poor. But she gave up gambling and con games to give me an honest, respectable life. And just look at the trouble I've caused her." She looked down at the floor. "I gambled at that poker game, and she had to sacrifice herself for me. Again."

He touched her cheek, forcing her to meet his gaze. "Josie." His eyes were deep and dark as a winter storm on a midnight sea. "The choice she made to sacrifice herself to my brother was not your fault. It was never your fault."

"Not my fault?" she repeated as, involuntarily, her eyes fell to his sensual lips. He seemed to lean towards her, and her own lips tingled, sizzling down her nerve endings with a strange, intense need. Somewhere in her rational mind, she heard a warning that she couldn't quite hear; her brain had lost all power over her body. Her traitorous heart went thump, thump in her chest. Still staring at his cruelly sensual mouth, she whispered, "How can you say it's not my fault?"

"Because I know your sister. And I know you." Cupping her face, he tilted her head back. "And other than my mother, who died long ago, I think perhaps you are the only truly decent woman I've known. And not just decent," he said softly. "But incredibly beautiful."

Josie's mouth fell open as she looked up. Her? Beautiful?

Was he—cripes—was it possible he was *flirting* with her?

Don't be ridiculous, she told herself savagely. *He's being courteous. Nothing more.* She had no experience with men, but she did know one thing: a devastatingly handsome billionaire prince would have no reason to flirt with a girl like her. But still, she felt giddy as she looked up at him, mesmerized by his blue eyes, which seemed so warm now, warm as a June afternoon, warm as one of the brief summers of her childhood in Alaska.

"Don't do that," he said.

"Don't what?"

"Look at me like that," he said softly.

She swallowed, lifting her gaze to his. "Then don't tell me I'm beautiful. It's…it's not something I've ever heard before."

"Then all the other men in the world are fools." His blue eyes burned through her. "Our marriage will be short, but for the brief time you are mine…" He put his hand over hers. "I am not going to stop telling you that you're beautiful. Because it's true." His lips curved up at the corners as he said softly,

"And didn't I just say that one should always speak the truth?"

Stop, Josie ordered her trembling heart as she looked up at his handsome face. There would be no schoolgirl crushes on her soon-to-be husband! Absolutely none!

But it was too late. The deed was done.

"Are you ready?"

"Ready?" she breathed.

He smiled, as if he could see the sudden brutal conquest of her innocent heart. "To marry me."

"Oh. Right." She bit her lip. "Um, yeah. Sure."

Pulling her into the foyer, he took a bouquet of white flowers out of a waiting white box. He placed a bridal bouquet in her hand. "For you, my bride."

"Thank you," she whispered, fighting back tears as she pressed her face amid the sweetly scented flowers.

He scowled. "Don't you dare tell me no man has ever given you flowers before."

She hesitated. "Well…"

"You're killing me," he groaned. "The men you know must be idiots."

She gave him a wan smile. "Well, I don't really know any men. So it would be unreasonable to expect them to buy me flowers."

"You don't know any men?" He stared at her incredulously. "But you're so friendly. So chatty."

"I don't talk to cute ones. I'm too nervous. Besides—" she gave her best attempt at a casual shrug "—Bree won't let me date. She's afraid I'll get hurt."

His lips parted. "You've never been on a date?"

She shook her head. "I did have a sort of boyfriend once," she added hastily. "In high school. We met in chemistry class. He was...nice."

"Nice," he snorted. "With your rose-colored glasses, he probably had a mohawk, a spiked dog collar and a propensity for stealing," he muttered.

"That's not fair," she protested. "After all, I think you're nice. And you're not a thief."

Looking uncomfortable, Kasimir cleared his throat. "Go on."

"We went out a few times for ice cream. Studied together at the library. Then he asked me to prom. I was so excited. Bree helped me fix up a thrift-shop dress, and I felt like Cinderella." She stopped.

"What happened?" he asked, watching her.

She looked away. "He never showed up," she whispered. "He took another girl instead, a girl he'd just met." She lifted her gaze in a trembling smile. "But she put out. And I...didn't."

A low growl came from the back of Kasimir's throat.

Clutching the bouquet of white flowers, Josie stared down at the pattern of the polished marble floor. "I just think kissing someone should be special. That you should only share yourself with someone you love." She shuffled her pink flip-flops, echoing the sound across the high-ceilinged foyer. "I expect you think it's stupid and old-fashioned."

"No." Kasimir's voice was low. "I used to think the same."

Her jaw dropped as she looked up. "What?"

He gave a humorless smile. "Funny story for you. I was a virgin until I was twenty-two."

"You?" Josie breathed. The fact that he'd told her something so intimate caused a shock wave through her. "The international playboy?"

He snorted. "Everyone has a first experience. Mine was Nina. She worked at a PR firm in Moscow, and we hired her to help our new business. She was far older than me—thirty. We dated for a few months. After I lost my half of Xendzov Mining, I went back to Russia to see her. I was floundering. I had some half-baked idea that I'd ask her to marry me." He gave her a crooked smile. "Instead, I found her in bed with a fat, elderly banker."

Josie gasped aloud.

He looked away. "I thought I was in love with her." He gave her a crooked smile. "Virgins usually think that, their first time. But Nina just thought of me as a client. To her, sex was 'networking.' And when I no longer was a potentially lucrative PR account, she no longer had reason to see me."

"Oh," Josie whispered. Her brown eyes were luminous with unshed tears. "I'm so sorry."

He shrugged. "She did me a favor. Taught me an important lesson."

She swallowed, looking up at him. "But just because one woman hurt you, that's no reason to give up on love forever."

His lips twisted sardonically. "You wouldn't say that if you'd seen me standing outside her apartment in the snow and ice, with an idiotic expression on my face."

"But—"

"You'll be my only wife, Josie. Because you're temporary. And this sham marriage will be over in weeks." Giving her a smile that didn't meet his eyes, Kasimir held out his arm. "Come, my beautiful bride," he said softly. "Our wedding awaits."

An hour later, Kasimir and Josie exchanged wedding rings, speaking their vows in a simple ceremony in the office of a justice of the peace in downtown Honolulu. Kasimir couldn't look away from the radiant beauty of his bride.

Or believe that he'd told her so much about his past. He'd told her about his first experience with love. He'd told her he'd been a virgin at twenty-two. What the hell had possessed him?

He didn't care if she looked at him with her weepy eyes and vulnerable smile. He'd never try to comfort her again with a little piece of his soul.

From now on, he'd keep his damned mouth shut.

"And do you, Josephine Louise Dalton, take this man to be your lawfully wedded husband, to have and to hold, in sickness and in health, for richer or poorer, as long as you both shall live?"

Josie turned to look at Kasimir, her soft brown eyes glowing as she whispered, "I do."

Kasimir's gaze traced downward, from her beautiful face to her slender neck, to those amazingly sexy curves in the tight, clinging white sheath.

And he'd keep his hands off her. His forehead burst out in a hot sweat as he repeated the rule to himself again.

He wasn't going to seduce Josie. He *wasn't*.

He had good reasons. All reasons he'd thought of before he'd seen her in this dress.

Who'd known she was hiding all those curves beneath her baggy clothes?

He'd nearly gasped the first time he saw her, when he'd been talking on the phone near his rooftop pool, tying up loose ends with Greg Hudson. The man was taking full credit for the way Bree Dalton and Vladimir had left together after the poker game, and wanted a bonus on top of the agreed-upon bribe. "I went to a lot of work," Hudson whined. "I didn't just hire the Dalton girls, I got them to trust me. And I managed to get your brother to leave with her. I think I deserve double." Kasimir had been rolling his eyes when he'd looked up and seen Josie in that tight white dress. "I'll talk to you later," he'd said, hanging up on the man in midsentence.

But he knew the whole story now. Bree had taken Josie's place at the poker table to try to win back her little sister's debt. She'd succeeded, and had been walking away from the table free and clear, when Vladimir had taunted her into one last game.

It was Bree's fault she was in Vladimir's hands. Her own pride had been her downfall.

And it irritated Kasimir beyond measure that Josie blamed herself for her sister's predicament. No wonder her father had established the land trust for her. She'd give undeserving people the very shirt off her back. She needed to be protected—even from her own soft heart.

Although he wouldn't mind taking the shirt off her back. He looked at the way her full breasts plumped above her neckline, and the white lace clung tightly to her tiny waist and hips. He looked at the curvaceous turn of her bare legs all the way to her casual pink flip-flops, and realized she might need to be protected from him, as well.

Because he wanted her in his bed.

He hadn't planned to want her, but he did. And seeing the glow of hero-worship in her big brown eyes made it even worse. It made him want her even more. She was so different from his usual type of woman. She wasn't sarcastic or snarky or ironic. Josie actually cared.

I just think kissing someone should be special. That you should only share yourself with someone you love.

She clearly had no idea how powerful lust could be. Her first experience would hit her like a tidal wave. It would be so easy to seduce her, he thought. One kiss, one stroke. She would be totally unprepared for the fire. But she would be an apt student. He felt that in the tremble of her hand as he slid the ten-carat diamond ring on her finger. Saw it in the rosy blush on her cheeks as she placed the plain gold band on his. All he would have to do would be to kiss her, touch her, and she'd be lost in a maelstrom of pleasure she would not know how to defend herself against. She'd fall like a ripe peach into his hands.

Except he couldn't. *Wouldn't.*

Unlike anyone else he'd met for a long while, Josie was a good person with a trusting heart. It was bad enough that he'd be virtually holding her hostage over the next few weeks in order to blackmail her sister and get revenge on his brother.

Kasimir could be ruthless, yes, even cruel. But to people who deserved it. Not to a sweet, trusting, old-fashioned young woman like Josie. She deserved better.

So he wouldn't take his wife to bed. He would control himself. No matter how difficult it might prove to be.

"I now pronounce you man and wife." Adjusting the flower lei around his neck, the officiant looked between them. "You may now kiss the bride."

With an intake of breath, Josie looked up at Kasimir with a tremulous smile.

He hesitated. It would be appropriate to kiss her, wouldn't it? It would almost be weird *not* to kiss her.

But he feared taking even one taste of what was forbidden. Undecided, he leaned forward, torturing himself as he breathed in the scent of her hair, like summer peaches. He wanted to wrap his hands in her hair, lower his mouth to hers and plunder those pink lips, and see if they were as soft and sweet as they looked...

He couldn't seduce her. *Couldn't.*

Kasimir turned his head, giving her a brief, chaste peck on the cheek, before he drew away.

She blinked, then reached for her bouquet, giving Kasimir a small smile, as if she were tremendously relieved he hadn't given her a proper kiss. As if she hadn't been waiting breathlessly for one.

Neither of them were glad he hadn't properly kissed her. Even the officiant looked bewildered as he cleared his throat. "Sign here," he told Kasimir's attorney, who was their witness. They posed for photographs, to make their wedding look real, and they were done.

"Get busy," Kasimir told his attorney, handing him the marriage license and the camera. "I expect the land in Alaska to be in my name before the end of January."

Today was December twenty-seventh. The man looked flummoxed beneath his wire-rimmed glasses. "But sir...the legal formalities of getting the trust to transfer the land to Miss Dalton, and then having her sell it to you are complicated. It could easily take three or four months...."

"You have four weeks," he cut the man off. Plenty of time to blackmail Bree Dalton into handing over his brother's company. And too much time of having Josie—now his wife—enticing him with her body and the latent passion in her deep brown eyes. The first man to take her might be consumed by it.

But it wouldn't be him. Kasimir set his jaw. He wouldn't touch her.

At all.

Even if it killed him.

"Kasimir?" Josie's brow furrowed. "What's wrong?"

She saw too much. "Nothing," he said shortly.

"Do you..." She paused, biting her lip. "You don't already regret marrying me...do you?"

"No," he said shortly. "I just don't want to make this marriage any harder for you than it has to be."

She glanced down at her Chanel gown, her beautiful bouquet, her enormous diamond ring. Her pink lips curved. "Well," she said teasingly, "this *has* been pretty tough to take."

"And I saved the best for last. Your cake."

"You didn't!" she cried happily. "What kind?"

"Three layers, with buttercream roses. You were sleeping, so I couldn't ask your favorite flavor. So each layer is different—white, yellow and devil's food."

Her eyes looked luminous. "You are so kind," she whispered.

He frowned at her.

"Don't you dare cry," he ordered.

"Don't be silly," she said, wiping her eyes. "Of course I'm not crying."

Kasimir cursed aloud. "How can the small kindness of cake make you weep?"

"You listened to me," she said, giving him a watery smile. "I'm not used to anyone actually listening to me. Even Bree just talks at me, telling me what I should want."

"No more. Remember, now you're a princess." He gave her a sudden cheeky grin. "Princess Josephine Xendzov." Reaching down, he stroked her cheek as he looked into her eyes. "Princess Josie, you're perfect."

"Princess." She gulped, then shook her head with a laugh. "If only the girls who teased me in high school could see me now!"

Setting his jaw, he looked down at her. "If any girls who teased you were here right now, I'd make them regret they were born."

Looking up at him, she gave a shocked laugh.

Then she blinked fast. She gave a sudden tearful sniff.

"Don't start that again," he said in exasperation. Grabbing her hand, he pulled her out of the justice of the peace's office and into the sunshine. The sky was a brilliant blue against the soaring skyscrapers of downtown Honolulu. Holding Josie's hand,

Kasimir led her to the Rolls-Royce waiting for them at the curb.

"Kiss her!" Some rowdy tourists shouted from a nearby bus, spotting him in a black suit and Josie with her white dress and bouquet, standing beside a chauffeured black Rolls-Royce.

Kasimir looked back at her. "They want me to kiss you."

Josie looked back at him breathlessly, her eyes huge with fear. "It's all right," she said awkwardly. "I know you don't want to. It's okay."

"Since this is my only wedding—" his hand tightened over hers as he pulled her closer "— this is my only chance to properly fulfill the traditions."

He felt her tremble in his arms, saw her lips part as she looked up at him, ripe for plunder. And he knew it would be easy, so easy, to possess her. Not just her lips, but her body. Her heart. Her soul.

"Josie," he said hoarsely, looking at her lips.

"Yes?"

He lifted his gaze. "You'll remember that our marriage is in name only. You know that. Don't you?"

Her cheeks went pale, and she dropped his hand with an awkward laugh. "Of course I know that. You think I don't know that? I know that."

"Good," he said, exhaling. Now he just had to keep on reminding himself. Turning away, he opened the door of the Rolls-Royce.

"I'm know I'm not your type," she chattered,

climbing into the backseat of the car. "Of course I'm not your type."

"No," he growled. He climbed in beside her as his chauffeur closed the door. "You're absolutely not."

Her lips tugged downward, and she abruptly fell silent. But as the Rolls-Royce drew away from the curb, she turned to him suddenly in the backseat with pleading eyes. "So what *is* your type?"

His type. Kasimir's jaw clenched. It was time to draw a line in the sand. To end the strange emotional connection that had leapt up between them since he'd told her about Nina. He'd never told anyone about that. But Josie had looked so sad, so vulnerable, he'd wanted to comfort her.

He'd overshot the mark. Because for the last hour she'd been looking at him as if he were some kind of damned hero just for some flowers and cake and sharing a story from his past. Enough. The way his body was fighting him now, he needed Josie to be on her guard against him. To remind them both that he was exactly what the world thought he was—a heartless playboy—he opened his mouth to tell her frankly about Véronique, Oksana and all the rest.

Taking her hand, Kasimir looked straight into her eyes.

Then he heard himself say huskily, "My usual type isn't half as beautiful as you."

He sucked in his breath. Why had he said that? How had it slipped past his guard? Was he picking up the habit from Josie—randomly blurting things out? He risked a glance at her.

Josie's jaw had dropped. Her hand trembled in his own. Her eyes were shining.

He pulled his hand away. "But I'm heartless, Josie. You should know I'm not the good man you think."

"You're wrong," she whispered. "I can tell—"

He turned away, clawing back his hair as he stared out the window at the passing city. "I don't want to hurt you," he said in a low voice. "But I'm afraid I will."

The truth was, he was starting to like the glow of admiration in her eyes. Josie had a good heart. He saw that clearly. But oddly, she seemed to think he had a good heart, as well—which was an opinion that no one on earth shared, not even Kasimir himself. But some part of him didn't want to see that glow in her eyes fade.

Although it would. Once she found out the truth about him, no amount of cake or diamonds or flowers would ever convince Josie to forgive the man who'd blackmailed her sister.

It doesn't matter, he told himself harshly. He was glad she admired him. That delusion would keep her close. She would have no reason to try to leave. Not that she could. Turning to her, he asked abruptly, "Why did you use your passport as ID for the wedding license? Don't you drive?"

She shook her head with a sigh. "Bree is too

afraid I'll get distracted by a sunset and crash, or forget where I parked, or maybe even give the car away to some beggar on the street. Not that we have a car," she said wistfully. "Our clunker that we drove south from Alaska died when we crossed the Nevada border."

"How can you not know how to drive?"

She bit her lip. "I would like to, but…"

"You are a grown woman. If you want to learn, learn. Nothing is stopping you."

"But Bree—"

"If she treats you like a child, it's because you still act like one. Mindlessly obeying her. I'm surprised she even let you get a passport," he said sardonically. "Isn't she afraid you might fly off to Asia and wreak havoc? Crash international stock markets in South America?"

She stared at him, wide-eyed. "How would I even do that?"

"Forget it," he bit out, looking out the window. "It just irritates me, how you've allowed her to control you. I can hardly believe you've bought into it for so long, looking up to her as if she's so much smarter than you, thinking that eventually, if you tried hard enough, you'd be able to earn her trust and respect—"

His voice cut off as he realized it wasn't Josie's sister he was talking about. Jaw tight, he glanced at her, hoping she hadn't noticed. His usual sort of mistress, who focused only on herself, wouldn't have registered a thing.

Josie was staring at him, her eyes wide.

"But Bree *is* smarter than me," she said in a small voice. "And it's okay. I don't mind. I love her just the same." She tilted her head. "Just as you love your brother. Don't you?"

Damn her intuitive nature. He turned away, his shoulders tight. "Loved. A long time ago. When I was too stupid to know better."

"You shouldn't give up on him. You should—"

"Leave it alone," he ground out.

"But you've spent the last ten years trying to destroy him—in this internecine battle—"

"Internecine?"

"Mutually destructive."

"Ah." His lips tugged up at the edges. "Well. Our rivalry has certainly been that. We've both lost millions of dollars bidding up the same targets for acquisition, sabotaging each other, planting rumors, political backstabbing. All of which Vladimir deserves. But I can hardly expect him just to take it without fighting back. No. In fact—" he tapped his knuckles aimlessly against the side of the car "—I'd have been very disappointed if he had."

"Oh," Josie breathed. "Now I get it."

Frowning, he looked at her. "Get what?"

"You're like little boys in some kind of quarrel, wrestling and punching each other till you're bloody. Till someone says 'uncle.' The reason you're fighting him so hard…is because you miss him."

Kasimir gave an intake of breath, staring at her. His shoulders suddenly felt uncomfortably tight. He was grateful when his phone rang. "Xendzov," he answered sharply.

"It's happened, Your Highness," his investigator said. "Even sooner than you expected. Your brother has started looking for Josie."

"Do you know why?" he bit out, extremely aware of Josie watching him anxiously in the back of the car.

"It could be at her sister's request. Or for some reason of his own. He tracked her commercial flight from Seattle to Honolulu. It's just a matter of time until he finds her on this island. With you."

Kasimir's hand tightened on his phone. "Understood."

"Who was that?" Josie asked after he hung up. "Was it about my sister?"

His lips tightened. "Change of plan." He turned to her. "We'll have to skip the cake."

"Did you find her?" she cried. "Where is she?"

"How would you like a surprise honeymoon?" he said evasively.

Josie scowled. "Why would I want that?"

Ouch. He tried to ignore the blow to his masculine pride. "You've never wanted to go to Paris?" he said lightly. "To stay at the finest hotels, to have a magnificent view of the Eiffel Tower, to shop in designer boutiques, to..."

His voice trailed off when he saw Josie shaking her head fiercely. "I just want my sister—home safe. As you promised!"

Kasimir sighed, telling himself they'd have been tracked to Paris, anyway, when he was surrounded by the inevitable paparazzi. He flashed her a careless smile. "Fine. No honeymoon."

"But do you know where Bree is?" she persisted.

"I might have a slight suspicion." It wasn't a lie. He knew exactly where Bree was, and he'd known since yesterday. She was at Vladimir's beachfront villa on the other side of Oahu. Too damned close for comfort. It was a miracle that for almost a week now, Kasimir had managed to keep it quiet that he was in Honolulu.

"Is she safe?" Josie grabbed his hand anxiously. "He hasn't—hurt her—in any way?"

Hurt her? Kasimir snorted. His investigator had seen Vladimir kissing her on a moonswept beach last night, while Bree, wearing a bikini, had been enthusiastically kissing him back. But at Josie's pained expression, he coughed. "She's fine."

"How can you know?"

"Because I know." Rubbing his throbbing temples, Kasimir leaned forward to tell his chauffeur, "The airport."

They'd already turned down the street of his penthouse as the driver nodded.

"Airport?" Josie breathed. "Where are we going?"

Kasimir smiled. "Let's just say I'm glad you have your passport..."

His voice trailed off as he saw Greg Hudson pacing on the sidewalk outside his building. He'd come to demand payment in person. A snarl rose to Kasimir's lips. *Damn his greedy hide.* If Josie saw her ex-boss, it would ruin everything. Intuitive as she was, she'd quickly figure out who'd bribed him to hire the two Dalton girls. And why. Then, married or not, she'd likely jump straight out of Kasimir's car, and that would be the end of his revenge.

Josie blinked. "Wait, are we back on your street?" She turned towards the chauffeur. "Could we please just stop for a moment at the penthouse, so I can pick up my bag before we go?" She glanced at Kasimir with a dimpled smile. "And I'll grab the cake."

The chauffeur looked at Kasimir in his rearview mirror, then said gravely, "Sorry, Princess."

"Tell him to stop," Josie said imploringly to Kasimir. She started to turn towards the window, her hand reaching instinctively for her door. In another two seconds, she'd see her ex-boss waiting outside the building, and Kasimir's plans would be destroyed.

He didn't think. He just acted. That was the reason, he told himself later, the only possible reason, for what he did next.

Throwing himself across the leather seat of the Rolls-Royce, he pulled her roughly into his arms.

He heard her gasp, saw her eyes grow wide. He saw panic mingle with tremulous, innocent desire in her beautiful face. He saw the blush of roses in her pale cheeks, breathed in the sweet peaches of her hair. His hands cupped her face as he felt the softness of her skin.

And then, with a low growl from the back of his throat, Kasimir did what he'd ached to do for hours.

He kissed his wife.

CHAPTER THREE

JOSIE TRULY DIDN'T believe he was going to kiss her. Not until she felt his mouth against her own. As he lowered his head to hers, she just stared up at him in shock.

Then she felt his lips against hers, rough and hot, hard and sensual as silk. She gasped, closing her eyes as she felt the caress of his embrace like a thousand shards of light.

In the backseat of the Rolls-Royce, Kasimir pulled her more tightly against him, and she felt his power, his strength. He tilted her head back, deepening the kiss as his hands twined in her hair. Her eyes squeezed shut as she felt the hot, plundering sweep of his tongue, felt the velocity of the world spinning around her, as if they were at the center of a sandstorm. She was lost, completely lost, in sensations she'd never felt before, in his lips and tongue and body and hands. When he finally pulled away, she sagged against him, dazed beneath the force of her own surrender.

But Kasimir just sat back against the seat, glancing out the car window calmly. As if he hadn't just changed her whole world—forever.

"Why…" she whispered, touching her tingling, bruised lips. "Why did you kiss me?"

Kasimir glanced back at her. "Oh, that?" He shrugged, then drawled, "The justice of the peace did tell me I was allowed to kiss you now."

Her heart was pounding. She tried to understand. "You did it to celebrate our wedding?" she said faintly. "Because you were overcome…by the moment?"

He gave a hard laugh. As the chauffeur drove the Rolls-Royce onto the highway, Kasimir looked away from her, as if he were far more interested in the shining glass buildings and palm trees and blue sky. "Exactly." His tone was sardonic. "I was overcome."

And she imagined she saw smug masculine satisfaction in his heavy-lidded expression.

Josie had never thought of herself as a violent person. If anything, she was the type to hide and quiver from conflict. But in this moment, she suddenly felt a spasm of anger. "Then tell me the real reason."

He looked at her. "You were handy."

She gasped. He hadn't kissed her to share the sacredness of the moment, or because he was overwhelmed by sudden particular desire for Josie. Oh, no. He'd kissed her just because she was *there*.

I'm heartless, Josie, he'd told her. *You should know I'm not the good man you think.*

Apparently he'd felt that words weren't enough

of a warning. He'd decided to show her, and this was exhibit A.

And for that, he'd ruthlessly stolen her first kiss away.

"It meant nothing to you?" she choked out. "You were just using me?"

"Of course I was," he said coldly. "What else could a kiss be? You know the kind of man I am. I don't do commitment. I don't do hearts and flowers and sappy little poems so dear to the innocent souls of tender little virgins," he ground out. His eyes were fierce as he glared at her. "So get that straight—once and for all."

She stared at him, her mouth wide-open.

Then emotion tore through her, like fire through dry brush. It was an emotion she barely recognized. She'd never felt it before.

Rage.

Hot burning tears filled her eyes. Drawing back her hand, she slapped his face—hard.

The ringing sound of the blow echoed in the car. Even the chauffeur in the front seat flinched.

Blinking in shock, Kasimir instinctively put his hand to his rugged, reddened cheek as he stared down at her.

"I dreamed about my first kiss for my whole life," she cried. "And you stole it from me. For no reason. Just to prove your stupid point!"

He narrowed his eyes. "Josie—"

"I get it. You don't want me to fall in love with

you. No worries about that!" A lump rose in her throat. "You turned a memory that should have been sacred into a mockery," she whispered. Tears spilled over her lashes as she looked away. "Don't ever touch me again."

Silence fell in the backseat of the limo. She waited for him to apologize, to say he was sorry.

Instead, he said in a low voice, "Fine."

She whirled to face him, eyes blazing. "I want your promise! Your word of honor!"

"You think I have a word of honor?" His handsome face was stark, his blue gaze oddly vulnerable as he looked down at her, his arms folded over his black vest and tie.

"Stop joking about this!" Her voice ended with a humiliating sob. "I mean it!"

Seeing her tears, he released his arms. He touched her gently on the shoulders.

"All right. I will never kiss you again," he said in a low voice. His blue gaze burned through her like white fire. "I give you my word of honor."

She swallowed, then wiped her eyes roughly with the back of her hand. "I don't like being used," she whispered. Squaring her shoulders, she looked up. "Just stick to our original deal. A professional arrangement. You get your land. I get my sister back safe."

"Yes." Matching her tone, he said, "We'll be at the airport in a few moments."

She suddenly remembered. "My backpack—"

"I'll have my housekeeper bring it to the airport."
Pulling out his phone, he dialed and gave his orders.
After he hung up, he asked Josie quietly, "What is
so important in the backpack, anyway?"

"Nothing much," she said, looking down at her
hands, now tightly folded over the white lace of her
dress. "An old photo of my family. A sweater that
used to belong to my mother. Before she—" Josie's
lip trembled "—died. Right after I was born."

Silence fell.

"I'm sorry," he said gruffly. "I lost my own mother
when I was twenty-two. I still miss her. She was the
only truly good, decent woman I've ever known. At
least until—"

His voice cut off.

"Until?"

"Never mind," he muttered.

Josie stared at him. Then her hand reached out
for his.

Kasimir looked down at her hand. "You're trying
to make me feel better?" he said slowly. He looked
up. "I thought you were ready to kill me."

"I was—I mean, I am." She swallowed, then
whispered, "But I know how it feels to lose your
parents. I know what it's like to feel orphaned and
alone. And I wouldn't wish it on my worst enemy."
She tried to smile. "Though I guess you've done
all right, haven't you? Being a billionaire prince
and all."

He stared at her for a long moment. "It's not always what it's cracked up to be." He looked away. "You asked me where we're going? I'm taking you home."

"To Alaska?"

He snorted, then shook his head. "Not even close." He looked down at her tight white dress. "We'll need to get you some new clothes."

She followed his gaze. Sitting down, her body was squeezed by the white sheath like a sausage, pressing her full breasts halfway to her chin. Her nipples were barely tucked in for decency. She gulped, fighting the urge to cover herself with her bouquet of flowers. She cleared her throat. "I was planning to wash all my dirty clothes today. Does this place we're going to happen to have a washer and dryer…?"

Her voice trailed off when she saw his gaze roaming from her breasts, to her hips, and back again. Her cheeks colored.

"I wish I'd never told you," she said grumpily, folding her arms and turning away.

"Told me what?"

"About the underwear."

Silence fell in the backseat of the car.

"Me, too," he muttered.

Josie craned her neck to look right, left, then up. And up some more.

"Unreal," she muttered.

Kasimir flashed her a grin. "I'm glad you like it."

"This is your *home?*"

"No." He smiled at her, looking sleek and shaved in a clean suit, having showered on their overnight flight. "My home is in the desert, a two-hour helicopter ride away. But this…" He shrugged. "It's just a place to do business. I come here as little as possible. It's a bit too…civilized."

Too civilized?

Josie shook her head as she looked back up at the beautiful Moorish palace, two stories tall, surrounded by gently swaying palm trees and the glimmer of a blue-water pool.

It was like a honeymoon all right, she thought. If you were really, really rich.

After sleeping all night on a full-size bed in the back cabin of Kasimir's private jet, she'd woken up refreshed. She'd looked out the jet's small windows to see a golden land rising beyond the sparkling blue ocean, and past that, sunlight breaking over black mountains.

"Where are we?" she'd breathed.

Kasimir had looked at her, his eyes shining. "Morocco." His smile was warm. "My home."

Now, they were standing in front of his palace in the desert outside Marrakech. She could see the dark crags of the Atlas Mountains in the distance, illuminated by the bright morning sun. Birds were singing as they soared across the wide desert sky. The pool glimmered darts of sunlight, like diamonds, against the deep green palm trees.

It was an oasis here. Of beauty, yes. She glanced behind her at the guardhouse beside the wrought-iron gate. But also of money and power.

"It's beautiful." She exhaled, then could no longer keep herself from blurting out, "So is she here?"

He looked at her blankly. "Who?"

"Bree." She furrowed her brow. "You said she was here!"

"I never said that. I said I had a slight suspicion of where she might be."

"Do you think she's in Morocco?"

His lips twisted. "Unlikely."

Josie glared at him. "Then why on earth did we come all the way here?"

"Hawaii was getting tiresome," he said coldly. "I wanted to leave. And I told you. This is where I do business…"

"Business!" she cried. "Your only business is finding Bree!"

"Yes." He tilted his head. "Once I have your land."

She gasped. "You said as soon as we were married, you'd save her!"

"No." He looked at her. "I said I'd save her *after* we got married. When I had possession of your land."

She shook her head helplessly. "You can't intend to wait for some stupid legal formalities…"

"Can't I?" Kasimir said sharply. "It would be easy for you to decide, after your sister is safely home, that you'd prefer not to transfer your land to me at all. Or to suddenly insist that I pay you, say, a hundred million dollars for it."

"A hundred million..." She couldn't even finish the number. "For six hundred acres?"

"You know what the land means to me," he said tightly. "You could use my feelings against me."

"I wouldn't!"

"I know you won't. Because you won't have the chance."

"Getting the land could take months!"

"I have the best lawyers in the country working on it. I expect to have it in my possession within a few weeks."

A few weeks? She forced herself to take a deep breath, to calm the frantic beating of her heart, so she could say reasonably, "I can't wait that long."

His lips pursed. "You have no choice."

"But my sister's in danger!" she exploded.

"Danger?" He looked at her incredulously. "If anyone's in danger, it's Vladimir."

Josie frowned. "What do you mean by that?"

He blinked. "She's always been his weakness, that's all," he muttered. He reached for her hand. "Come inside. I want to show you something."

He led her through the exotic green garden towards the palace, and as they walked past the soaring Moorish arches, she looked up in amazement. The foyer was painted with intertwined flowers and vines and geometric motifs in gold leaf and bright colors. Raised Arabic calligraphy was embedded into the plaster on the walls. She'd never seen anything quite so beautiful, or so foreign.

Josie's lips parted as, in the next room, she saw the ornamental stucco pattern of the soaring ceiling, which seemed to drip stalactites in perfect symmetry. "Are those *muqarnas?*" she breathed.

He looked at her with raised eyebrows.

"I love architecture coffee-table books," she said, rather defensively.

"Of course you do." He sounded amused.

Her eyes narrowed, and she tilted her head. "It's beautiful. Even though it's fake."

"Fake?" he said.

"The builder tried to make it look older, Moorish in design, but with those art-nouveau elements in the windows…I'm guessing it was built in the 1920s?"

He gave her a surprised look. "You got all that from a single coffee-table book?"

Her cheeks colored slightly. "I might have spent a few hours lingering over books at my favorite couscous restaurant."

He grinned at her. "Well, you're right. This was built as a hotel when Morocco was a French protectorate." He looked at her approvingly. "There's no way Bree is smarter than you."

Her heart fluttered. In spite of her best efforts, she was still beaming foolishly beneath his praise as he led her past a shadowy cloistered walkway to the open courtyard at the center of the palace. The white merciless sun beat down in the blue sky, but the center courtyard garden was cool, with lush flowers and an orange tree on each corner. Soft breezes sighed through palm trees, leaving dappled shadows over the burbling stone fountain.

"Josie?" Kasimir was staring at her.

She realized she'd stopped in the middle of the courtyard, her mouth open. "Sorry." Snapping her lips shut, she followed him across the courtyard to a hallway directly off the columned stone cloister.

He held a door open for her.

"This will be your room," he murmured. She walked past him to find a large bedroom with high ceilings, sumptuously decorated, with two latticed windows, one facing the courtyard, the other the desert. "You will need something to wear while you're here."

"No, really," she protested. "All I need is a washer and a dryer—"

He opened a closet door. "Too late."

Peeking past him, she saw a huge closetful of women's clothes, all with tags from expensive designers. She said doubtfully, "Whose are these?"

"Yours."

"I mean, where did they come from? Were they… left here by your other, um, female guests?"

"Female guests." His lips quirked. "Is that what you call them?"

"You know what I mean!"

"I wouldn't come all the way to Marrakech for a one-night stand." His smile lifted to a grin. "Why would I bother going to the trouble?"

"Yeah, why," she muttered. Her husband could seduce any woman with a smile. He'd melted Josie into an infatuated, delusional puddle with a single careless, stolen kiss.

She scowled. "Look. I just want to know if I'm wearing clothes you bought for someone else."

He gave an exaggerated sigh. "They were purchased in Marrakech for you, Josie. Specifically for you. And if you don't believe me..." He gave her a wicked grin as he opened a drawer. "Check this out."

Her lips parted as she looked down at all the lacy unmentionable undergarments.

"You'll never have to go commando again," he said smugly. His eyes met hers. "Unless you want to."

She swallowed, then turned away as her cheeks burned. "Great... Thanks."

"And for your information," he said behind her, "I would never bring a female guest here."

She didn't meet his eyes. She was afraid he would notice how she was trembling. "I'm the first?"

"Ah," he said softly. "But you're more than a guest." Reaching over, he tucked a tendril of her hair off her face. "You are my wife."

As his fingertips stroked her skin, she felt his nearness, felt his powerful body towering over hers.

Swallowing, she turned away, pretending to look through the expensive items in the closet to hide her confusion.

"Well?" he said huskily. "Do you see anything you like?"

Her heart gave an involuntary throb as she looked back at him.

"Yes," she said in a low voice. "But nothing that's right for me."

His blue eyes narrowed as he frowned. "But they're your size."

"That's not what I meant."

"Then what?"

She swallowed. "Look, I appreciate the gesture, but…" She stopped herself in her tracks, then blurted out, "They're all just too—fancy."

He drew back, blinking in surprise. "Too fancy?"

She nodded. "I like clothes I can be comfortable in. Clothes I can work in."

He looked at her. "But you wore that all night?"

She looked down at her tight wedding dress. "Well. I just put this back on. I slept naked."

Kasimir swallowed. "Naked?" he said hoarsely.

"Look, I really appreciate your sweet gesture, but until I can wash my own clothes, couldn't I just borrow some of your old jeans?" she said hopefully. "Maybe an old T-shirt?"

The shock on his handsome face was almost comical. "You'd rather wear my old ratty work clothes than Louis Vuitton or Chanel?"

Not wanting to examine too carefully the reasons for that, she just nodded.

He snorted. "You're a very original woman, Josie Xendzov."

Josie Xendzov. Her heart did that strange thump-thump again. "So people have always told me."

"So what work are you planning to do around here, Princess? Dig trenches in the dirt? Change the oil in my Lamborghini?"

"You have a Lamborghini?" she said eagerly.

His lips curved. "You don't give a damn about designer clothes, but you're impressed by a car? You can't even drive!"

She shrugged. "My father had a Lamborghini when I was six years old. He had it shipped up to Alaska, delivered to our house in the middle of winter. The roads were covered with snow. Impossible to drive the Lamborghini with those wide performance tires."

Kasimir nodded. "You'd slide right into a snowbank."

"So Dad let me pretend to drive it in the driveway. For hours. I remember it was dark, except for flashes of the northern lights across the sky, and I drove the steering wheel so recklessly. Pretending to be a race-car driver. We both laughed so hard." She blinked fast. "It was the first time I ever really heard him laugh. Though I heard he used to laugh all the time before my mom died." She looked down at her feet. "I miss my family," she whispered. "I miss my home."

For a moment, he didn't move.

Then his warm, rough hands took her own. With an intake of breath, she looked up, waiting for him to tell her Black Jack Dalton had been a criminal who didn't deserve a Lamborghini. She waited for Kasimir to mock her grief, to tell her she should put the memory of childhood happiness away, like outgrown toys, discarded and forgotten.

Instead, Kasimir put his hand on the small of her back, pulling her close as he looked down at her.

"So you have a fondness for Lamborghinis, do you?" he said softly, searching her gaze. "They're not too fancy?"

Josie looked up at his ruggedly handsome face. Every inch of her body felt his touch on her back. She shook her head. "Nope," she whispered. "Not fancy."

"In that case…" With a wicked smile, he reached out to stroke her cheek as he said softly, "I know just what I'm going to do with you."

CHAPTER FOUR

Two hours later, Josie's body was shaking with fear.

Her hand trembled on the gearshift. "I can't believe you're making me do this."

"I'm not making you do anything."

She'd changed out of her tight dress, but in spite of wearing Kasimir's old rolled-up jeans and a clean, slightly tattered black Van Halen T-shirt, she didn't feel remotely comfortable. She'd showered, too, but that hadn't done her much good, either. Her forehead now felt clammy with sweat. The two of them were in the enormous paved exterior courtyard of the palace. In his Lamborghini.

And for the first time since she was a child, Josie was in the driver's seat.

"You wanted to learn how to drive," Kasimir pointed out.

"Not in your brand-new Lamborghini!"

"Snob, huh? So it's suddenly 'too fancy' for you after all?"

"You're laughing now. You'll be crying when I crash it straight into your pool."

He shrugged. "I'll buy a new one."

"Car or pool?"

"Either. Both."

She gaped at him. "Are you out of your mind? These things cost real money!"

"Not to me." Reaching over, he put his hand on her denim-clad leg. She nearly jumped out of her skin before she realized he was only pressing on her knee. "Push down harder on the clutch. Yes." He put his other hand over hers on the gearshift. "Move it like that. Yes," he said softly as he guided her. "Exactly like that."

Josie gulped, her heart pounding in her throat. She accelerated, then stalled. She stomped on the gas, then the brakes. She spun out, again and again, kicking up clouds of dust.

"You're doing great," Kasimir said for the umpteenth time, even as he was coughing from the dust. He gave her a watery smile, his face encouraging.

"How can you be so patient?" she cried, nearly beating her head against the steering wheel. "I'm terrible at this!"

"Don't be so hard on yourself," he said gruffly. "It's your first time."

Resting her head against the steering wheel, Josie looked at him sideways. Since she'd met Kasimir, it had been her first time for lots of things. The first time she'd ever been recklessly pursued by a man who wanted to marry her. The first time she'd felt her heart pound with strange new desire. The first time she'd ever been wildly, truly infatuated with anyone.

She looked down at the huge diamond ring on her finger, seeing the facets flash in the light. The first time she'd fully realized the depths of her bad luck, that she was married to a handsome prince, whose secretly kind heart would unfortunately never pound that way over her.

Never ever, her brain assured her.

Not in a million years, her heart agreed.

His phone rang, and he looked down at the number. "Excuse me."

"Sure," she said, relieved to take a break from driving, or whatever her tire-screeching, bloodcurdling version of driving might be. She stretched in her seat, yawning.

Then she noticed how Kasimir had turned his body away from her to speak quietly into the phone. He got out of the car altogether, closing the door behind him.

Who on earth was he speaking to? Josie's eyes narrowed. Clearly someone he didn't want her to know about. Was it information about Bree? Or—cripes, could he be talking to another woman, making plans for a romantic getaway as soon as he was safely rid of her?

She quietly got out of the driver's-side door.

Kasimir had turned away to speak into the phone.

In a very low voice. *In Russian.* "My brother's private jet left for Russia? You're sure?" He paused. "And she's still with him? Very well. Get out of Oahu and head for St. Petersburg. As soon as you can."

Hanging up, Kasimir turned around. His eyes widened as he saw her standing beside him in the dust-choked driveway.

"What was that about?" she asked casually.

"Nothing that concerns you."

"You haven't found my sister?"

"Nope." He gave her a careless, charming smile. Lying to her. Lying to her face! "You've almost got the clutch down. Ready for more?"

She didn't move. "I studied Russian in school," she ground out. "For six years."

His expression changed.

"You found Bree," she whispered, hands clenching at her sides. "She was on Oahu. And you didn't want me to know."

Kasimir stared at her, then resentfully gave a single nod.

Closing her eyes, Josie took a deep breath as grief filled her heart. "She was on Oahu. All the time we were there, we could have just driven across the island at any time and picked her up?"

"If we'd gone the moment you arrived at my penthouse—yes." Her eyes flew open. His cold blue gaze met hers. "We weren't married then. You could have walked away. I had no reason to tell you."

With a little cry, Josie leapt towards him. She pounded on his chest. "You bastard!"

He didn't move, or try to protect himself. "I don't blame you for being angry," he said softly.

"So that's why you brought me here?" Wide-eyed, she staggered back. "Damn you," she whispered. "How selfish can you be?"

He looked at her. "You already know the answer to that, or else you're a fool."

But she was. She was a fool, because she'd believed in his compliments and lies! Turning on her heel, she started to walk away.

He grabbed her wrist, turning her to face him. "Where do you think you're going?"

"To St. Petersburg," she flashed. "To save her, since you won't!"

"And just how do you intend to do that?" He sounded almost amused. "With no money and nothing to barter?"

She tossed her head. "Perhaps your brother is interested in trading for his old family homestead!"

She heard his ragged intake of breath. "You couldn't do that."

"Why not? It's mine now. Thanks for marrying me."

His hand tightened on her wrist. "That land belongs to me—"

"I signed a prenup, remember? It protected all your possessions and fortune you brought into our marriage. But it also protected mine!"

His blue eyes were like fire. "You—you, the last honest woman—would try to steal my land? And give it to my brother?"

"Why not? You stole my first kiss!" she cried, trembling all over. She looked away, blinking fast. "It should have been something special, something I shared with someone I loved, or might love someday. And you ruined it!" She turned on him fiercely. "You lied to my face from the moment I came back to Honolulu. You won't go save Bree until you legally get my land? You say you can't trust me? Fine!" She tossed her head. "Maybe I won't trust you, either!"

His expression was dark, even murderous. "Yes. I lied to you about your sister's whereabouts. And yes, kissing you was a mistake." His grip on her wrist tightened as he looked down at her. "But don't act like a traumatized victim," he ground out. "You enjoyed our kiss. Admit it."

"What?" She tried to pull away. "Are you crazy?"

He wrapped her in his arms, bringing her tight against his hard body. "Claim what you want. I know what I felt when you were in my arms," he growled. "I felt your body tremble. You looked at me with those big eyes, holding your breath. Parting your mouth, licking your lips. Did you not realize you were giving me an invitation?" Cupping her face, he glared at her. "It is the same thing you are doing now."

She swallowed, yanking her chin away as she closed her mouth with a snap. She blinked fast.

"Maybe I did want you to kiss me. *Then*," she whispered. Wistfully, she looked towards the wrought-iron gate, towards the road to the Marrakech airport. "But I don't anymore. All I want now is for you to let me go."

For a moment, the only sound was the pant of her breath.

"Is being married to me really so awful?" he said roughly. "Was—kissing me—really so distasteful to you?"

She took a deep breath.

"No," she said honestly. She couldn't lie. She pushed away from him. "But I can't just wait around here for weeks, hoping she's all right. If you're in no hurry to save her…I'll make a deal with someone who is."

"You'll never even make it to Marrakech."

"I'll hitchhike into town," she tossed back. "And hock my wedding ring for a plane ticket to St. Petersburg."

"You'll never even be able to talk to him!"

She stopped. "My phone," she breathed aloud. "I'll call my sister's number. Either she will answer it, or Vladimir will. The battery is dead but I'll plug it in and…" Triumphantly, Josie glanced behind her. Then she saw his face.

With a gasp, she started to run towards the house. She was only halfway across the inner courtyard, racing for her bedroom, when he came up behind her, scooping her up with a growl. "I won't let you call him."

She struggled in his arms. "Let me go!"

"Vladimir will never have that land." Beneath the swaying palm trees of the sunny courtyard, next to the soft burbling water of the stone fountain, he slowly released her, and she felt the strength of his muscular form as she slid down his body. He gripped her wrists. "It's mine. And so are you."

She shook her head wildly. "You can't keep me prisoner here. I'll scream my head off! One of your servants will..."

"My servants will say nothing. They are loyal."

It was impossible to pull her wrists out of his implacable grip. Tears filled her eyes.

"Someone will talk," she whispered. "Someone will hear me. We're not that far from the city. I'll find a phone that works. Or email. There's no way you can keep me here against my will."

Kasimir looked down at her, then his eyes narrowed. He abruptly let her go.

"You're right."

She rubbed her wrists in relief. "You're letting me go?"

His sensual mouth curled in a devastating smile. He looked every inch a ruthless Russian prince, his blue eyes icy as a Siberian winter. "Wrong," he said softly.

Frightened of the coldness in his eyes, Josie

slowly backed away. "Whatever you're planning, it won't work. I'll escape you..."

Their eyes locked, and shivers went through her. "Will you?" he purred.

And coiling back like a tiger, he sprang.

Kasimir heard the loud whir of the helicopter flying away as he stood on thick carpets over the packed sand in his own grand tent, the largest and most luxurious in his camp, deep inside the Sahara Desert.

He looked down at his prisoner—that is to say, his dear wife—sitting on his bed. Tied up with a soft silken gag over her mouth, Josie was glaring at him with bright sparks of hatred in her eyes.

His eyes traced down her body. She still wearing his black T-shirt and oversized jeans from Marrakech, but from the flash of lacy bra strap, he knew she was wearing the sexy lingerie he'd given her underneath. His body tightened. He said softly, "What am I going to do with you?"

Josie answered him in a muffled, angry voice, and he had the feeling she was telling him what he should do with *himself,* and that her suggestion was not a courteous one.

Kasimir sighed. He should have guessed Josie might speak Russian—it was sometimes taught in Alaskan schools. He regretted that he'd let himself be caught in such a clumsy lie.

But at the moment, he regretted even more his promise never to kiss her again. A word of honor was a serious thing: unbreakable. He'd unknowingly broken a vow once, to his dying father, when Vladimir had sold their homestead behind his back. Kasimir wouldn't break another.

The truth was he'd been attracted to Josie Dalton from the moment they'd met on Christmas Eve, in the Salad Shack. Kissing her in the back of his Rolls-Royce yesterday, far from satiating his desire, had only made him want her more. Her shy, trembling, perfectly imperfect kiss had punched through him like a hurricane, knocking him over and sucking him down beneath the sensual undertow of her sweet, soft embrace.

Why did she have such power over him?

He felt a sudden hard thwack against his shin.

Exhaling, Kasimir looked down at her, sitting on his bed. "Stop trying to kick me, and I'll untie you."

"Mmph!" Josie responded angrily. If looks could kill, a lightning bolt would have sizzled him on the spot, leaving only the ash of his body to be carried away like smoke on the hot desert wind.

With a sigh, he reached down and untied the white sash from her mouth. "I warned you what would happen if you didn't stop screaming," he said regretfully. "You were driving the pilot crazy. Tark's been in some rough places, flown military missions all over the world. But even he had never heard the kind of curses that came shrieking out of your mouth."

Her mouth now free, Josie coughed. "You kidnapped me, you—" And here she let out a torrent of new invective against his manhood, his intelligence and his lineage in her sweet Sunday-school voice, that left him wide-eyed at her creative vulgarity.

"Ah, my dear." He gave a soft laugh. "I'm beginning to think you are not quite the innocent I thought you were."

"Go to hell!"

He tilted his head. "Who taught you to swear like that?"

"Your *mother,*" she bit out insultingly. Then with an intake of breath, Josie looked up, as if she'd just remembered that his mother had died. She bit her lip, abashed. "I'm sorry," she said in a small voice. She held out her wrists. "Would you mind please untying me now?"

Kasimir stared at her. After the way he'd thrown her bodily into his helicopter, ignoring her protests, tying her up—she felt guilty for her single thoughtless insult? She was afraid of causing *him* pain?

Bending to untie her wrists, he muttered, "You are quite a woman, Josie Xendzov."

"So you keep telling me." She looked around his enormous, luxurious white canvas tent, from the four-poster bed to the luxurious Turkish carpets lining the hard-packed sand floor. A large screen of carved wood covered the wardrobe, illuminated by the soft golden light of a solar-powered lamp. "Where are we?"

"My home. In the Sahara."

"Where in the Sahara?"

"The middle," he said sardonically.

"Thanks." Narrowing her eyes she tossed her head. "I'm grateful you're not just going to leave me in chains. As your prisoner."

"It's tempting," he said softly. "Believe me."

As he loosened the knots around her wrists, he tried not to notice the alluring softness of her skin. Tried not to imagine how the white lacy bra and panties looked beneath her clothes. Tried not to think how easy it would be to push her back against his bed, to stretch back her arms, still bound at the wrists, against the headboard. To press apart her knees, still bound at the ankles. He tried not to think how it would feel to lick and caress up her legs, to the inside of her thighs, until he felt her tremble and shake.

No. He wouldn't think about it. At all.

A bead of sweat broke out on Kasimir's forehead. *His word of honor.* That meant his lips and tongue couldn't possibly yearn to suckle her full, ripe breasts. His hands could not ache to part her virgin thighs. He couldn't hunger to stroke and kiss her until he lost himself deep, deep, deep inside her hot wet core.

The bindings on her wrists abruptly burst loose and, as the rope dropped to the floor, Kasimir took a single staggering step back from her. He ran his hand over his forehead, feeling dizzy.

She rubbed her free wrists, looking up at him dubiously. "Are you all right?"

Blinking, he focused on her beautiful brown eyes, expressive and still slightly resentful, in the fading afternoon light. Her voice was like the cool water of an oasis to a man half-dead with thirst. Did she feel the same electricity? He'd been so sure of it in Honolulu. In Marrakech, he'd been absolutely confident of the answering desire in her eyes. But now, he wondered if that had just been a mirage in the desert, an illusion created by his own aching, inexplicable need.

Josie took a deep breath. "Please," she whispered.

"Yes," he said hoarsely. He wanted to please her. He wanted to push her back against the pillows and rip the clothes from her body. He wanted to thrust himself inside her until he felt her scream and explode with joy.

"Please—" she held out her ankles "—finish untying me."

Kasimir exhaled. "Right," he said unsteadily.

Holding himself in check, he knelt at her feet. From where she sat on the bed, her long legs were stretched towards him, her heels on the Turkish carpet. Even in the baggy jeans he'd loaned her, she had legs like a houri—the pinnacle of feminine beauty. As he undid the ropes, his fingertips unwillingly brushed against her calves, against the tender instep of her sole. He felt her shiver, and he stopped, his heart pounding. He looked up her legs, straight past her knees to her thighs, and the heaven that waited there, then to her breasts, then to her face. His body broke out into a hot sweat.

His word of honor.

With a twist and a rip, he yanked the rope off her ankles. His own legs trembled as he rose to his feet. He clenched his hands at his sides, his body tight and aching for what he could not have.

"I shouldn't have tied you up," he said in a low voice. "I should have told Tark to go to hell and just let you scream curses at me for two hours."

"No kidding." She stared at him, waiting, then she gave a crooked smile. "So are you going to say you're sorry?"

"Mistakes were made," he said tightly, and that was the best he could do.

Her smile widened. "You're not used to saying you're sorry, are you?"

"I don't make it a habit."

"Too bad for you. It's a big habit with me. I say it all the time. You should try it."

"It's been a while." Kasimir's throat burned as he remembered the last time he'd apologized. Ten years ago, he'd arrived in St. Petersburg to discover his "interview" was all over the business news. He'd immediately phoned his brother, still in Alaska. Kasimir still writhed to remember the pitiful way he'd groveled. *I'm sorry. I didn't know he was a reporter. Forgive me, Volodya.*

But his brother had just used his confession

against him, convincing Kasimir his mistake was a betrayal and they should end their partnership immediately. And all along Vladimir had secretly known a billion-dollar mining deal in Siberia was about to come through.

"How long has it been since you apologized?" Josie asked softly.

Kasimir shrugged. Saying sorry was tantamount to admitting fault, and he'd learned that humbly asking for forgiveness was a useless, self-destructive exercise, like flinging your body in front of a speeding train. It could only end in being flattened. "Ten years."

Her jaw dropped. "Seriously?"

"I have to go." His shoulders felt tight in his suit jacket. "Just stay here, all right? I'll be back in a few minutes."

"Where are you going?"

"To change out of these clothes. And take a quick shower." From the corner of his eye, he saw her immediately glance at her old backpack on the floor. He could almost see the wheels turning in her mind. Fine, let her dig for her phone. Let her try to use it out here—with no way to recharge the dead battery and no connection even if she'd had power. He looked back at her. "Make yourself comfortable. But don't try to leave the encampment," he warned. "You're in the middle of the desert. There is no way for you to escape, so please don't try."

"Right." Josie nodded, her expression blank and bland. "No escape."

"I mean it," he said sharply. "You could die a horrible death, lost in the sand."

"Die a horrible death. Got it."

With a sigh, he tossed back the heavy canvas door, and went to a nearby smaller bathing tent. He knew Josie was up to something, but she'd soon see there was nowhere to go. He twisted his neck to the left, cracking his vertebrae. She'd hopefully spend the next ten minutes trying to get her phone to work. He gave a low laugh.

Taking off his suit, he used silver buckets filled with cool, clean water to wash the grime of civilization off his skin. He exhaled, feeling his shoulders relax, as they always did here. He changed into the traditional male caftan over loose-fitting pants. His body felt more at ease in a lightweight djellaba than he'd ever felt in a suit. He loved the natural wildness of the desert, so much more rational and merciful than the savage corporate world.

As he left the bathing tent, Kasimir looked up at the endless blue sky, at the white-sand horizon stretching to eternity. There were eight large white tents, most of them used by his Berber servants who maintained this remote desert camp, surrounding the deep well of an oasis. On the edge of the camp was a pen for the horses, and farther away still, a helicopter pad. He'd given up trying to drive here. He'd destroyed three top-of-the-line Range Rovers trying to drive over the sand dunes before he'd finally given up on driving altogether and turned to horses and helicopters.

Now, he looked across the undulating sand dunes stretching out to the farthest reaches of the horizon. Sand muffled all sound at this lonely spot on the edge of the Sahara. The sun was falling in the cloudless blue sky.

His oasis in the desert was as far from Alaska as he could possibly get. He had no memories here of the bleak, cold snow. Or of the only promise he'd ever broken.

Yet.

Kasimir sighed. He was starting to think it was a mistake to wait until he had the land before he searched for Bree. Not just because it was making Josie so unhappy, but also because it was growing agonizing for him to be near his wife and unable to touch her.

"Sir." One of his most trusted servants, a man in a blue turban, spoke to him anxiously in Berber. He pointed. "Your woman…"

Kasimir's lips parted as he saw Josie struggling up a nearby dune, kicking off her flimsy flip-flops, her bare feet sinking in the sand to her knees.

A sigh escaped him. He should have known that mere warnings of death wouldn't be enough to stop Josie from trying single-handedly to rush off to save that sister of hers. Irritated, he went after her.

Catching up with her easily, he grabbed her hand

and pulled her all the way to the top of the dune. Then he abruptly released her.

"Look where you are, Josie," he raged at her. "Look!"

With an intake of breath, Josie turned in a circle, looking in every direction from the top of the dune. It was like standing in the middle of an ocean, surrounded by endless waves of sand.

"There's a reason why I brought you here," he said quietly. "There is nowhere for you to go."

She went in circles for five minutes before the truth of his words sank in on her, and she collapsed in a heap on the sand. "I can't stay here."

Kasimir knelt on the sand beside her. Reaching out, he tucked some hair away from her face. "I'm still going to save your sister. So stop trying to run away," he said gruffly. "Okay?"

Wiping her eyes, she sat on the sand, looking at him. "You can't just expect me to just sit here and do nothing, and leave her fate in Vladimir's hands. Or yours!"

"I thought you said I was a good man with a good heart."

She hiccupped a laugh, then sniffled. "I changed my mind."

His jaw tightened. "Your sister is in no danger. Vladimir has done nothing worse to her than making her scrub the floor of his villa."

"How do you know?"

"His housekeeper in Hawaii was not pleased to see him treating a female guest so rudely. But Bree has always been my brother's weakness. That is why I—" *Why I arranged for them to cross paths in Hawaii,* he almost said, but cut himself off. He could hardly admit that now, could he? Josie's trust in him was on very tenuous ground already. He set his jaw. "I've just found out he has her at his palace in St. Petersburg, where his company is busy with a merger."

"And he's not—bothering her?"

His lips curved. "From what I've heard, her greatest suffering has involved too much shopping at luxury boutiques with his credit card."

Josie frowned. "But Bree hates shopping," she said uncertainly.

"Maybe you don't know her as well as you think." He stood up, then held out his hand. "Just as she does not truly know you."

She put her hand into his. "What do you mean?" she said softly.

"She's spent the last decade treating you like something fragile and helpless. You are neither." He pulled her up against him, looking down at her. "You are reckless, Josie. Powerful. Fearless."

"I am?" she breathed, looking up into his eyes.

"Didn't you know?" He searched her gaze. "You risk yourself to take care of others. Constantly. In a way I cannot imagine."

She bit her lip, looking down.

His hand tightened on hers. "No more escape attempts. I mean it. I swear to you that she is safe.

Just be patient. Stay here with me. From this moment, you will be treated not as a prisoner, but as an honored guest."

"*Honored guest?* You said I was more."

"I cannot treat you as my wife," he said huskily. "Not anymore."

"What do you mean? Of course you…"

"I cannot make love to you." His eyes met hers. "And since we kissed in Honolulu, it's all I can think about."

He heard her intake of breath.

"But I gave you my word of honor. I will not touch you. Kiss you. Make love to you for hours on end." Kasimir's larger hand tightened over hers. He looked down at her beautiful face, devoid of makeup. Her luminous brown eyes were the sort a man could drown in. And her lips… He shuddered. "You are safe, Josie," he whispered. "Until the end."

She slowly nodded. Holding her hand, he turned to lead her down the dune. They walked sure-footedly down the spine of sand, pausing to collect her discarded shoes, until they reached the encampment below. He thought about the cake he'd ordered for her, left behind in Honolulu. He'd order a wedding feast for her tonight. He would do everything he could to treat her as a princess—as a queen. That much he could do.

At the door of his tent, he glanced back to tell her how he planned to make her evening a happy one. Then he saw how her shoulders were slumped in his old black T-shirt, how the jeans he'd loaned her had unrolled at the hem, to drag against the ground. Her face was sad.

Something twisted in Kasimir's chest.

He suddenly wanted to tell her he was sorry. Sorry he'd brought her here. Sorry he'd dragged her into his plans for revenge. And sorry above all that when she discovered the blackmail against her sister, it would be a crime that even Josie's heart would be unable to forgive. She would despise him—forever. And he was starting to realize hers was the one good opinion he'd regret.

But when he opened his mouth to say the words, they caught in his throat.

Clenching his jaw, he turned away, pointing at the wardrobe. "You have fresh clothes here." He gestured towards the large four-poster bed, the sumptuous wall-to-wall Turkish carpets. "I will ask the women to bring you refreshment and a bath. When you are done, we will have dinner." He gave her a smile. "A wedding feast of sorts."

But she didn't smile back. She didn't seem interested, not even in the bath—a rare luxury in the desert. Sitting down heavily on the edge of the bed, she lifted her gaze numbly.

"I don't want to stay here with you," she whispered. She was so beautiful, he thought. His gaze traced from her full, generous mouth down the curve of her long, graceful neck. Like a swan. So unself-conscious, as if she had no idea about her beauty, about the way her pale skin gleamed like cream in the shadows of the tent, or the warmth and kindness that caused her to glow from within, as if there were a fire inside her.

And that fire could be so much more. Standing beside the bed, he felt how alone they were in his private tent. He could push her back against the soft mattress and see the light brown waves of her hair fall like a cascade against the pillows. He could touch her skin, stroke its luminescence with his fingertips and see if it was as soft as it looked.

He had to stop thinking about this. Now.

Kasimir turned away, stalking across the tent. He flung open the heavy canvas flap of the door, then stopped. Standing in the late-afternoon sun, he heard the sigh of the wind and the distant call of desert birds. Shoulders tight, without turning around, he said in a low voice, "I never should have kissed you."

He heard her give a little squeak. He slowly turned back to face her.

"I was wrong." He took a deep breath. And then, looking into her shocked brown eyes, he spoke the words he hadn't been able to say for ten years. "Josie," he whispered, "I'm sorry."

CHAPTER FIVE

AN HOUR LATER, Josie was in the tent, bathed, comfortable and wearing clean clothes. And more determined than ever to escape.

Okay, so her phone didn't work and her impulsive escape attempt had been laughable. But she couldn't stay here. Whatever Kasimir thought, she couldn't just be patient. She had no intention of abandoning Bree for weeks in her ex-boyfriend's clutches and trusting all would be well.

Why had Kasimir even insisted on keeping her here? There was no reason he couldn't have her sign some kind of letter of intent or something, promising to give him the property. Something just didn't add up. She felt as if she'd become almost as much a prisoner as Bree was. Two prisoners for two brothers, she thought grimly.

And yet...

Josie brushed her long brown hair until it tumbled softly over her shoulders. Somehow, he'd also made her feel free. As if she, of all people, could be daring enough to travel around the world, learn to drive on a Lamborghini and boldly catch a powerful man in a lie.

You are reckless, Josie. Powerful. Fearless.

Could he be right? Could that be the voice inside her, the one she'd ignored for so long, the one she'd been scared to hear?

Dropping the silver-edged brush, she pulled her hair back into a ponytail. Well, she was listening to it now. And that meant one thing: maybe she would have accepted being in a cage once…

But she'd be no man's prisoner now.

Josie stood up in her pale linen trousers and a fine cotton shirt she'd found in the wardrobe, in her exact size. She'd just come back from the bathing tent, where she'd been delightfully submerged in hot water and rose petals. As she'd watched the Berber servants pour steaming water into the cast-iron bathtub, she'd felt as though she was in another century. In *Africa.* In Morocco.

"He's called the Tsar of the Desert," one of the women had whispered. "He came here with a broken heart."

Another woman tossed rose petals into the fragrant water. "But the desert healed him."

A broken heart? *Kasimir?* If she hadn't already heard his story about his lost love, Josie would have found that hard to believe. With a shiver, she pictured him, all brooding lips and cold eyes…and hard, broad-shouldered, muscular body, towering over her. A man like that didn't seem to have feelings. She would have assumed he didn't have a heart to break.

But now she knew too much. An orphan who'd been stabbed in the back by his beloved older brother. A romantic who'd waited to lose his virginity, then fallen for his first woman, even planning to propose to her. If she'd known Kasimir when he was twenty-two...

Josie shivered. She would have fallen for him like a stone. A man with that kind of strength, loyalty, integrity and kindness was rare. Even she knew that.

She knew too much.

Now, as she left his tent, she looked out at the twilight. *Stop having a crush on him,* she ordered herself. She couldn't let herself get swept up in tenderness for the young man he'd once been—or in desire for the hard-eyed man he'd become. She couldn't get caught up in the romance of the desert, and start imagining herself some intrepid lady adventurer from a 1920s movie matinee. Kasimir was *not* some Rudolph Valentino-style sheikh waiting to ravish her, or love her.

No matter how he'd looked at her an hour ago.

I never should have kissed you. I was wrong. Josie, I'm sorry.

She pushed away the memory of his haunted voice, and hardened her heart. She couldn't completely trust him—no matter how handsome he was, or how he made her feel. There was something he wasn't telling her. And she wasn't going to stick around to find out what it was.

The air was growing cool in the high desert. She saw the darkening shadows of dusk lit up by torches on both sides of the oasis. It looked like magic.

She'd find a chance to escape. And this time, she wouldn't just run off. She'd figure out a plan. She'd seen horses on the edge of the encampment. Perhaps she could borrow one. She'd never been much of a planner. Bree had the organized mind for that. Josie was more of a seat-of-your-pants type of girl.

She'd figure it out. She'd seize her chance. Sometime when Kasimir wasn't looking.

Josie looked for him now, turning her head right and left. She pictured his handsome face, so intense, so ruthless. No wonder, under the magnetic force of his complete attention, she'd once felt infatuated—at least before she'd realized he was a liar and kidnapper. Her brief crush wasn't anything to be embarrassed about. With Kasimir's chiseled good looks, electric-blue eyes and low, husky voice— and the sensual stroke of his practiced fingertips, rough against her skin—any woman would have felt wildly attracted. But her crush was over now. Her hands tightened. She wasn't going to let him stop her from doing what she needed to do.

But it couldn't hurt to be fortified with dinner before her escape. Her stomach growled. Calories would give her energy, which would give her ideas.

Josie looked around for the dining tent. The sun was setting at a rapid pace.

A man in an indigo turban bowed in front of her. "Princess," he said in accented English.

Princess…? She blushed. "Oh. Yes. Hello. Could you please tell me where Kasimir—Prince Kasimir—might be?"

The man smiled then gestured across the encampment. "You go, yes? He waits."

"Yes, of course," she stammered. "I'll hurry."

Josie went in the direction he'd pointed. She wasn't sure she was going the right way, until she suddenly saw a path in the sand, illuminated by a line of torches in the dusk.

She followed the path, all the way up the spine of the tallest sand dune. At the top, she discovered a small table and two chairs on a Turkish carpet, surrounded by glimmering copper lanterns.

Kasimir rose from one of the chairs. "Good evening." Coming forward, he bent to kiss her hand. She felt the heat of his lips against her skin before he straightened to look at her with dark, sizzling blue eyes as he said huskily, "You look beautiful."

She gulped, pulling back her hand. "Thank you for the clothes, and the bath," she said weakly. "I hope you haven't been waiting long."

He gave her a warm smile that took her breath away. "You are worth waiting for."

Silhouetted in front of the red-and-orange twilight, Kasimir looked devastatingly handsome in the long Moroccan djellaba with its intricate embroidery on the edges and loose pants beneath. His head was bare, and the soft wind ruffled his black hair as he pulled back her chair. "Will you join me?"

Holding out her chair was such an old-fashioned, courtly gesture. And in this setting, with this particular man, it was extremely romantic. In spite of her best efforts, a tremble rose inside her. *I do not have a crush on him anymore,* she told herself firmly, but apparently her legs hadn't gotten the message, because they turned to jelly.

She fell into her chair. He pushed it back beneath the table, and as she felt his fingertips accidentally brush her shoulders, she couldn't breathe. She didn't exhale until he took his own seat across the small table.

"How lovely," she said, looking around them. "I never would have thought a table could be brought up here. It's enchanting...."

"Yes," he said in a low voice, looking at her. "Enchanting."

Their eyes locked in the deepening twilight, and spirals of electricity traveled down Josie's body to her toes, centering on her breasts and a place low and deep in her belly. Looking at the hard angles of his chiseled face, she felt uneasy. She suddenly wanted to lean across the table, to touch and stroke the rough dark stubble of his jawline, to run both her hands through his wind-tousled black hair....

What was she thinking? Nervously, she looked

down at the flickering lanterns that surrounded the carpet. She was relieved to see four servants with platters of food coming up the path illuminated by torches in the dusk.

"I've ordered a special dinner tonight that I hope you'll enjoy," her captor said softly. "Would you care for some white wine?"

She gulped. "Sure," she said, trying to seem blasé, as if drinking wine in the Sahara with billionaire princes was something she did every day. Oh, good heavens. With her billionaire prince *husband*.

Pouring wine from a pitcher into a crystal-and-gold goblet, he handed it to her. Smoothly, she lifted it to her lips. She didn't much like the smell, but she took a big drink anyway.

Then she sputtered, and nearly choked. Making a face, she pulled the glass away from her lips.

"Don't you like it?" Kasimir asked in surprise.

"Like it?" She blurted out. "It tastes like juice that's gone bad!"

He laughed, shaking his head. "But Josie, that's exactly what wine is." He tilted his head, giving her a boyish grin. "Though I don't think the St. Raphaël winery will be using those exact words in their ads anytime soon. No wine, huh?"

"I didn't like it."

"I never would have guessed. You hide your emotions so well."

For an instant, they smiled at each other, and Josie's heart suddenly twisted in her chest. Then, turning away, he lifted his hand in signal. "I'll get you something you'll like better."

He spoke in another language—Berber?—to one of the servants, and the man left. After serving their dinner, the other three, too, departed, leaving Kasimir and Josie to enjoy a private dinner in the Sahara, beneath the shadows of red twilight.

"Ooh." Looking down at the table, Josie saw a traditional Moroccan dinner, full of things she loved: *tajine,* a zesty saffron-and-cumin-flavored chicken stew—pickled lemons and olives, carrot salad sprinkled with orange-flower water and cinnamon and couscous with vegetables. She sighed with pleasure. "You have no idea how often I ate at the Moroccan restaurant, trying to imagine what it would be like to travel here."

"How often?"

"Every time I got my hands on a half-off lunch coupon."

He grinned at her, then the smile slid from his face. His expression grew serious.

"So," he said in a low voice, "does that mean you forgive me? For bringing you here?"

She looked in shock at the vulnerability in his eyes. Something had changed in him somehow, she thought. The warm, generous man sitting across from her in exotic Moroccan garb seemed very different from the cold tycoon in a black suit she'd met in Hawaii. Had the desert really made him so different? Or was it just that she knew too much about the man behind the suit?

"I don't like that you lied to me about Bree," she said slowly. "Or that you brought me out here against my will. But," she sighed, taking a bite of the *tajine* as she looked at the sunset, "at the moment it's a little hard for me to be angry."

He swallowed. Reaching across the table, he briefly took her hand. "Thank you."

She shivered as their eyes met. Then he released her as the servant returned with a samovar of filigreed metal. He left it on the table in front of Kasimir, then disappeared.

"What's that?" Josie said, eyeing it nervously.

He smiled. "You'll enjoy it more than wine. Trust me."

She wrinkled her nose. "I'd enjoy anything more than that," she confessed.

"It's mint tea."

"Oh," she sighed in pleasure. She watched him pour a cup of fragrant, steaming hot tea. "This is kind of like a honeymoon, you know."

He froze. "What do you mean?"

"The bath with rose petals. This wonderful dinner. The two of us, in Morocco. It's like something out of a romantic movie. If I didn't know better, I would have thought…"

Whoa. She cut herself off, biting down hard on her lower lip.

He looked up from the samovar. "You'd have thought what?"

"You were trying to seduce me," she whispered.

His shoulders tightened, then he shrugged, giving her a careless smile belied by the visible tension in his body. "I could only dream of being so lucky, right?" He swept his arm over the horizon, over the tea and the lanterns, with a sudden playful grin. "You can see the tricks I'd use to lure you."

"And I'm sure they'd work," she said hoarsely, then added, "Um, on someone else, I mean." Looking away quickly, she changed the subject. "How did you find this place?"

He set down the elegant china cup on the table in front of her. Sitting back in his chair, he took a sip of his own wine. "After Nina dumped me, I had the bright idea that I should go see every single place where I held mining options. After our partnership dissolved, I still held the mining rights in South America, Asia and Africa." He gave her a crooked smile. "Vladimir was happy to let those lands go. He didn't believe I'd ever find anything worth digging."

"But you proved him wrong."

"Southern Cross is now a billion-dollar company, almost as wealthy as his." His lips curved. "I left St. Petersburg with total freedom—no family, no obligations, almost no money, nothing to hold me back. Every young man's dream."

"It sounds lonely."

He took a drink from his crystal goblet. "I bought a used motorcycle and got out of Russia, crossing through Poland, Germany, France, Spain—all the way to the tip of Gibraltar. I caught a ferry south to Africa, then in Marrakech, I took roads that were barely roads—"

"You wanted to disappear?" she whispered.

He gave a hard laugh. "I did disappear. My tires blew up, my engine got chewed up by sand. I was dying of thirst when they—" he nodded towards the encampment "—found me. Luckiest day of my life." He took another gulp of wine. "They call this place the end of the world, but for me, it was a beginning. I found something in the desert I hadn't been able to find anywhere."

"What?"

He put his wineglass down on the table and looked at her. "Peace," he whispered.

For a moment, they both looked at each other, sitting alone on an island amid an ocean of sand in the darkening night.

"What would it take to make you give up the war with your brother?" Josie asked softly.

"What would it take?" His eyes glittered in the deepening shadows. "Everything that he cares about."

"It's just so...sad."

He looked at her incredulously. "You're sad? For him? For the man who took your sister?"

She shook her head. "Not for him. For you. You've

wasted ten years of your life on this. How much more time do you intend to squander?"

He finished off his wine in a gulp. "Not much longer now."

The brief, cold smile on his face made her shiver. "There," she breathed. "That smile. There's something you're not telling me. What is it?"

Kasimir stared at her for a long time, then turned away. "It's not your concern."

She watched the flickering shadows from the lanterns move like red fire against his taut jaw. He clearly wanted to end the subject. *Fine,* she told herself. What did she care if Kasimir wasted his life on stupid revenge plots? She didn't care. She *didn't.*

She bit her lip, then said hesitantly, "Is hurting your brother really more important to you than having a happy life yourself?"

"Leave it alone, Josie," he said harshly.

Josie knew she should just be quiet and drink her mint tea but she couldn't stop herself from replying in a heated tone, "Maybe if you just talked to him, explained how he'd hurt you—"

"He'd what, apologize?" Kasimir ground out. "Give me back my half of Xendzov Mining, wrapped in a nice gold bow?" His lips twisted. "There must be limits even to your optimism."

She looked up quickly, her cheeks hot. "You keep telling me to be honest, to be brave and bold, but what have you done lately that was any of those things?"

He looked at her.

"If I weren't bound by my vow," he said, "I'd do the bravest, boldest, most honest thing I can think of. And that's kiss you."

She sucked in her breath.

Exhaling, Kasimir looked up, tilting his head back against his chair. "Look at the stars. They go on forever."

Josie stared at him, her lips tingling, her heart twisting in her chest. Then she slowly followed his gaze. He was right about the stars. They had never looked so bright to her before, like twinkling diamonds above a violet sea. Looking at them, she felt so small, and yet bigger, too, as if she were part of something infinite and vast.

"You really want to kiss me so badly?" she heard herself say in a small voice.

"Yes."

"And it's not just because I'm—handy?"

He groaned. "I never should have said that. I knew I was wrong to kiss you. I was trying to act like it was no big deal." His lips quirked upward. "Hoping maybe you wouldn't notice that it was."

Her own lips trembled. "Oh, I noticed."

Their eyes locked across the table. As they faced each other, alone in the desert, the full moon had just lifted above the horizon. The world seemed suspended in time.

"But why me?" she choked out. "You could kiss

any woman you wanted. And we both agreed I'm not your type...."

Tilting his head, Kasimir looked at her. "You keep talking about my type. What is my type?"

She looked down at her plate, which had been filled with enough *tajine* and bread for your average Moroccan lumberjack. It was now empty—and just a moment ago, she'd been considering going back for seconds. She bit her lip. "She's thin and fit. She spends hours at the gym and rarely eats anything at all."

He gave a slow nod. "Go on."

Josie looked down at her linen trousers and plain cotton blouse that had felt so good, but now seemed dowdy and dumpy. "She's very glamorous. She wears tight red dresses and six-inch stiletto heels." She ran a hand over her ponytail. "She has her hair styled every single day in a top salon." She pressed her bare lips together. "And she wears makeup. Black eyeliner and red lipstick."

He gave her a crooked smile. "Yes. Even when I wake up beside her in bed, her lipstick is perfectly applied."

"What, you mean when you wake up in the morning?" Josie blinked, pulled out of her reverie. "How is that even possible? Do magic makeup fairies put lipstick on her in the middle of the night or something?"

He lifted a dark eyebrow. "Obviously, she gets

roat ached with pain. "You don't have to sugar-oat it. I'm chubby."

"Chubby?" He shook his head. "You drove me insane in your wedding dress. You taunted me in that sliver of white lace, teasing me with little flashes of your breasts and thighs until I thought I'd go mad." Standing up, he walked around the table. "You have the type of figure that men dream about," he said quietly. "And if you haven't noticed, I'm a man."

Kasimir stood over her now, so close their bodies almost touched. Her body sizzled as her lips parted.

"But I'm plain," she whispered. "I'm naive and silly. I blurt out things no one cares about."

He knelt beside her chair. "Your beauty doesn't come from a jar." He took her hand gently in his own. "It comes from your heart."

His palm and fingertips were warm and rough against hers. And Josie suddenly realized that he wasn't just being courteous. He wasn't trying to give compliments to an honored guest. He wasn't even flirting, not really.

He actually believed what he was saying to her.

A lump rose in her throat. How she'd longed to hear those words from someone, anyone, let alone a devastatingly handsome man like Kasimir....

But she couldn't let herself fall for it. *Couldn't*. She swallowed. Her voice was hoarse as she said, "I'm nothing special."

"Are you joking?" His hand tightened over hers. "How many women would have spent their last

up early, to freshen up her makeup and hair
I wake up."

Josie dropped her fork with a clang against
plate. "Sheesh! What a waste of time!" She thou,
of how much she loved sleeping in on mornin,
she didn't have to work. And if she happened to b
sharing a bed with a man—a man like Kasimir—
there surely would be better ways to wake up. Not
that she would know. Her cheeks flared with heat
as she pushed away the thought. She scowled, folding her arms. "You would never know the flaws of
a woman like that. So long as she's wearing lots of
lipstick and a tight red dress, you don't really know
her at all."

Kasimir stared at her in the moonlight.

"You're right," he said softly. "And that's why I
want you."

Josie dropped her folded arms. "What?"

"More than I've ever wanted any woman." He sat
forward in his chair, his eyes intense. "I know your
flaws. They're part of what makes you so beautiful."

She swallowed, looking down as she mumbled,
"I'm dowdy and frumpy."

"You don't need sexy clothes for your natural,
effortless beauty."

"I'm a klutz." She looked down at her empty
plate, feeling depressed. "And I eat too much."

"You eat the exact right amount for your perfect
body."

"My what?" She gasped out a laugh, even as her

money to cross an ocean—and agree to marry a man like me—just to save an older sister who's perfectly capable of taking care of herself?"

Josie's whole body was shaking. With an intake of breath, she pulled away. "Anyone would have—"

"You're wrong." He cut her off. "And that is what's different about you. You're not just brave. Not just strong. You don't even know your own power. You are— " he kissed the back of her hand, causing a flash of heat across her body as he whispered "—an elemental force."

Her body felt as if it was on fire. A breeze blew through the desert night, cooling her skin. Her heart pounded in her chest. She looked up at him.

The wind caught at his black hair, blowing it against his tanned skin, against his high cheekbones that looked chiseled out of marble in the silver moonlight and flickering glow of the lanterns.

"Now do you understand? Now do you believe?" he said softly. "I want you, Josie. Only you."

He reached out to stroke her cheek, and the sensuality of that simple touch caused her whole body to shake. Against her will, her gaze dropped to his mouth. Could she…? Did she dare to…?

Kasimir's hand dropped.

"But I will be true to my word. And I am almost glad you bound me by it." He gave her a small, wistful smile. "Because we both know that you are far too good for a heartless man like me."

Searching his gaze, she swallowed. "Kasimir—"

His expression shuttered. "You are tired." Rising to his feet, he held out his hand. "I will take you back to the tent."

But Josie didn't feel tired. Every sense and nerve in her body was aware of the stars, the night, the desert. From a distance, she could hear the call of night birds. She breathed in the exotic scent of spice on the soft warm wind. She'd never felt so alive before. So awake.

Because of him.

Kasimir's handsome face was frosted by moonlight, giving his black hair and high cheekbones a hard edge of silver. He looked like a prince— or a pirate—from a far-off time. Euphoria sang through her body, through her blood. *Like an elemental force.*

As if in a trance, Josie reached for his hand. Without a word, he led her down the sand dune towards the encampment. She was distracted by the feel of his hand against hers, by the closeness of his powerful body. Her feet were somehow as sure-footed as his as they walked lightly over the sand, down past the flickering torches blazing through the night, illuminating their path.

Kasimir led her into his private tent. They faced each other, and as they stood beside the enormous four-poster bed, which suddenly seemed to dominate the luxurious tent, Josie's knees felt weak. Her lips felt dry, her heart was pounding.

He looked down at her with smoldering eyes, as

if only a hair's breadth kept him from pushing her back against the bed and covering her body with his own. As if some part of him were waiting—praying for her to say the magic words: *Kasimir, I release you from your promise.*

Josie clenched her hands into fists at her sides. And, in a supreme act of will, stepped back from him.

"Well," she choked out. "Good night."

He tilted his head, frowning. "Good night?"

"Yes," she stammered. "I mean, thank you for our wedding night. I mean, our wedding feast. It was delicious. I'll never forget how you tasted—I mean, how the *tajine* tasted." *Oh, for heaven's sake.* Squaring her shoulders, she cried out, "But good night!"

"Ah." His sensual mouth curved at the edges. He took a step towards her. Josie almost lifted her arms to push him away. That was surely the reason she yearned to put her hands against his chest, to touch the powerful plane of his muscles through his djellaba and see if they could possibly be as hard as they looked. "Josie," he murmured, "I don't think you understand." He leaned his head down towards her with a gleam in his eye. "This is my private tent."

She licked her lips. "And you're giving it to me as your guest? No." She shook her head. "I couldn't possibly accept. I'm not kicking you out of your bed."

"Thank you." His eyebrow lifted as he said evenly, "And I'm not going to allow you to run away."

"What?" She jumped, flushed with guilt. "What makes you think I'm planning to run away?"

He put his hand over his heart in an old-fashioned gesture, even as his eyes burned through her. "If you run out into the desert alone, you will die in the sand."

She swallowed nervously. "I would never…"

"Then give me your word." In the dim light of the tent, lit by only a single lantern, his gaze seemed to see straight through her soul. He put his hand on her cheek.

"My word?" she echoed softly.

"As I gave you mine. Not just a promise. But your sacred word of honor—" his eyes met hers "—that you won't try to leave."

She sucked in her breath, knowing what a word of honor meant—to both of them. Her cheeks were burning as she licked her lips. "What would be the point? Do you really think I'm that much of an idiot to—"

"I think you are an incurable optimist. And when it comes to people you love, you make reckless decisions with your heart. I cannot allow you to put yourself at risk. So I intend to sleep here. With you. All night."

"Here?" she squeaked. She frantically tried to regroup, to think of a way she could still try to escape. Maybe if she waited until he was deeply asleep in the middle of the night… She licked her lips. "So you're going to sleep where—on those pillows? Or on the carpet, across the doorway of the tent?"

"Sorry. I'm not sleeping on the floor." Coming closer to her, he smoothed a tendril of hair off her face, looking down at her with something like amusement. "Not when I have a nice big bed."

She furrowed her brow, then with an irritated sigh, she rolled her eyes. "You mean after all that song and dance about me being your honored guest, you want the bed, while I get the floor?" She folded her arms, scowling.

Then she saw a spot on the floor not too far from the door. He was actually doing her a favor. She brightened. This would be almost too easy! Looking up, she saw his suspicious, searching glance, and tried to rearrange her own face back into a glower. She tossed her head, pretending she was still really, really mad. "Fine. I'll sleep on the floor like a prisoner. Whatever."

"I'm afraid that solution is also unacceptable," Kasimir said gravely, looking down at her with his midnight-blue eyes. "There is only one way I can make sure you do not try to sneak out in the night the moment I am asleep."

She stared at him in dawning horror.

"We are going to share this bed," he said huskily.

CHAPTER SIX

"No way!" Josie exploded. "I'm not sharing a bed with you!"

She folded her arms and stuck out her chin, glaring at Kasimir in a way that told him everything he needed to know.

He'd been right. She'd been planning to escape.

Narrowing his eyes, Kasimir folded his arms in turn and glared right back at her. "If I cannot trust you, I will keep you next to me all night long."

She now looked near tears. "You're being ridiculous!" She unfolded her arms. "Can't you just trust me not to escape?"

His eyebrow lifted. "Sure. I told you. All you need to do is give me your word of honor."

Her eyes widened, and then her shoulders sagged as she looked away.

"I can't," she whispered.

Kasimir brushed back some long tendrils of light brown hair that had escaped her ponytail. "I know."

Her brown eyes were bright with misery as she looked back at him. "How did you guess?"

"Ah, *kroshka*." He looked down at her trembling pink lips, at her cheeks that were rosy with emotion. "I can see your feelings on your face." His jaw tightened. "But you saw how deep we are in the desert. Even with your reckless optimism, you cannot think that running away on foot in the middle of the night is a good idea."

"That wasn't my plan," she mumbled.

"If you try to flee, you'll die. You'll be swallowed up by the desert and never be found again."

Her shoulders slumped further, and she wouldn't meet his eyes. "I wouldn't..." She took a deep breath, then lifted her eyes, shining with unshed tears that hit him like a knife beneath his ribs. "I just can't share a bed with you," she whispered.

His hands clenched.

"Damn you, can't you understand?" He had to restrain himself from shaking her. "It's either share a bed with me, or I'll tie you up as you were before, and leave you to sleep on the floor!"

She didn't answer.

"Well?" he said sharply.

"I'm thinking!"

He exhaled, setting his jaw. "I'm not going to seduce you. Surely you know that by now. What more can I do to prove it to you?"

"You don't have to do anything," she said in a small voice. "I believe you."

"Then what are you so afraid of?"

She looked at him in the dim light of the flickering lantern as they stood alone together in his tent.

"But what if I touch you?" she whispered.

Kasimir's whole body went hard so fast he nearly staggered back from the intensity of his desire. He held his breath, staring down at her as he choked out, "You—"

"Just accidentally, I mean," she said, her cheeks red. "I might roll over in bed in the middle of the night and put my arms around you while I'm sleeping. Or something. You might wake up and, well, get the wrong idea…"

The wrong idea? Kasimir's mind was filled with dozens of ideas, and all of them seemed exactly *right*. He looked at the way she was chewing her full, pink lower lip. A habit of hers. He wanted to lean forward and taste its sweetness for himself. To part her mouth with his own and stroke deep inside with his tongue. To push her back against the blue cushions of the bed, to feel her naked skin against his, and bury himself deep inside her.

"Well, would you?" she said awkwardly. "Or would you know it was all…an innocent mistake?"

Kasimir cleared his throat, forcing the seductive images of her from his mind. "You don't need to worry," he said, hoping she didn't notice the hoarseness of his voice. "I do not make a habit of pouncing on virgins in the middle of the night."

She stared at him, then gave him a sudden, irrepressible smile that caused a dimple in her cheek. "Why? Is there some other time you prefer to do it?"

She was teasing him! His lips parted in surprise, then he gave a low laugh, shaking his head. "For your information, I've never been anyone's first lover."

Josie blinked. "Ever?"

"No," he said softly. "You were my first 'first' kiss."

"I was?"

"And I've changed my mind," Kasimir said in a low voice. "I'm not sorry about kissing you. Because I'll never forget how it felt."

For an instant, they looked at each other in the flickering light.

"Nor will I," she whispered.

The night wind shook noisily against the canvas of the tent, and he forced himself to turn away. "Change for bed."

"Change clothes in the same tent? Forget it!"

"You can change behind the screen. I won't look."

"Can't you please wait outside?"

"And give you the chance to run off in the dark? No."

"But I don't have a nightgown." She choked out a nervous laugh. "Am I supposed to sleep naked?"

Naked. He squeezed his eyes shut, imagining the full, bare curves of her naked body, hot and smooth beneath his hands. He shuddered, his body aching.

He realized he had clenched his hands again. His fists were as hard as the rest of him.

Stop it, he ordered his body, which ignored him. He exhaled.

"Look in that trunk." He waved his hand behind him without looking towards her. "Over there. They should fit."

"Really? Thanks." He heard her go to the trunk and dig through it before she went towards the wooden screen painted with designs of flowers. "I guess I owe you."

"You can pay me back by not getting yourself killed," he growled, still not turning around. "What was your plan of escape, anyway?"

"My plan?" When he heard her voice muffled behind the screen, he knew it was safe to turn around. He saw her arms lifting over the top of the painted wooden panels as she pulled off her shirt. She tossed it over the screen, followed by the white lacy bra he'd given her. He swallowed, feeling hot. She gave a low laugh. "You're right, it was completely stupid. I hadn't figured out the exact details, but I was going to steal a horse from your pen, fling myself on it and ride bareback into the sunset."

"Do you have experience with horses?"

"Absolutely none." She tossed her pants over the top of the screen with a merry laugh. "Now that I'm considering my plan in a more rational light, I'm kind of relieved you figured it out."

Josie was naked behind the screen—or nearly so,

just wearing the lacy white panties he'd had purchased for her in Marrakech. He tried not to think about it. Because in a moment, they'd be lying beside each other in his big bed.

He had the sudden feeling that it was going to be a long night.

"Pretty nightgown," she mused behind the screen. "And modest, too."

He was grateful for that, although in his current state of mind he knew he'd be aroused by her even if she was covered from head to toe. Turning away, he pulled off his djellaba, leaving his chest bare, wearing only his lightweight, loose-fitting pants. "Just so you know," he said, "I generally sleep in the nude."

He heard her gulp.

"But not tonight," he said quickly.

"Good." She breathed an audible sigh of relief. "I've never seen a naked man before, and tonight doesn't seem like the time to start."

He couldn't even disguise the hoarseness of his voice this time. "Never?"

Lifting on her tiptoes, she peeked over the screen, looking at him over the painted wooden panels. Her eyes lingered over his bare chest as she purred, "Never."

Kasimir didn't breathe till she ducked back behind the screen. Her arms lifted as she pulled the nightgown over her head. The loose fit of his pants had never felt so uncomfortably tight before.

"Is it safe to come out?" she called.

"Safe as it will ever be," he muttered.

Josie came around the screen in a silver silk nightgown, bias-cut in a retro style, which went to her ankles, but left her arms bare. "Thanks for this. It's very retro. Nineteen forties."

"I told my staff to ransack the vintage shops, and avoid designer boutiques. Warned them not to get all 'fancy.'"

"I love this." She stroked the silk over her belly. "It's…soft."

His fingers itched to discover that for himself. He didn't let himself move. "Glad you approve."

Their eyes met. His forehead broke out into a sweat. At the same moment, they both abruptly turned towards the water basin, causing their hands to brush.

Josie ripped back her hand as if he'd burned her. "You go ahead."

"No, be my guest."

"All right." Keeping a safe distance, she quickly washed her face and brushed her teeth, then walked a semi-circle around him towards the bed. She was afraid to touch him, which meant she felt the same electricity, after all. Knowing she wanted him made this all the harder.

Or maybe it was just him.

As he brushed his teeth, out of the corner of his eye he watched her climb into bed, watched the silk of her nightgown move as sensuously as water over her curves. Putting down his toothbrush, he splashed cold water on his face, wishing he could drench his whole body with it.

Josie hesitated, biting her lip prettily as she glanced at him. "Do you care which side—"

"No," he ground out.

She frowned. "You don't have to be so rude…"

He looked at her, and something in his face made her close her mouth with a snap. Without another word, she jumped into bed and pulled the covers all the way up to her chin.

"Ready." Her voice was muffled.

He put out the flickering lantern light. Stretching his tight shoulders, he climbed in beside her. They each took opposite sides of the bed in the darkness, neither of them moving as the wind howled against the canvas roof.

"Kasimir?" her soft voice came from the darkness a moment later. "What will you do…when all this is over?"

"You mean our marriage?"

"Yes."

He leaned his head back against the pillow, folding his arms beneath his head. "I'll have everything I ever wanted."

"You mean the land?"

He exhaled with a flare of nostril. "Among other things."

"But you're not planning to live in Alaska, are you?"

Live at the old homestead? He inhaled, remembering nights sharing the cold attic room with his brother. Remembering the constant love of his hard-working parents, and how he'd bounded up eagerly each morning to start his chores.

As a boy, Kasimir had felt so certain of what mattered in the world. Home. Family. Loyalty.

"No, I won't go back," he said quietly.

"Then why do you want it so badly? Just because of your promise to your father?"

"It was a deathbed vow…" He stopped. He'd told himself that same lie for years, but here in the darkness, lying in bed beside her, he couldn't tell it again. "Because I don't want Vladimir to have it. He doesn't deserve a home. Or a brother."

"What about you?" Josie said softly. "What do you deserve?"

Kasimir looked away from her, towards his brief-case, which looked distinctly out of place in the corner of the tent. "Exactly what I will get," he said. Retribution against his brother and the Mata Hari who'd caused their rift. Total ownership of both Xendzov Mining and Southern Cross. That would make him happy. Give him peace.

It would. It had to. Looking at her shadowy form in the darkness, he turned the question back on her. "What will you do? With your life?"

"I don't know." She swallowed. "Bree always talked about sending me to college, but even if we had the money, I'm not sure that's what I want."

"Why not? You'd be good at it."

She gave a regretful laugh. "Bree should have been the one to go. She's a planner. A striver. Though she dropped out of high school to help support me." He could hear the self-blame in her voice. Then she laughed again. "But maybe she was glad. She was impatient with school. She's always had an eye to the bottom line. If not for those old debts threatening us, she'd be running her own business by now."

"I didn't ask about Bree's dreams," he said roughly. "I asked about you. What do *you* want?"

She paused. "You're going to think it's stupid."

"Nothing you want is stupid," he said, then snorted. "Except maybe stealing my horse and riding off alone into the desert."

"Not one of my best ideas," she admitted. For a long moment, they lay silently beside each other in the darkness. Kasimir started to wonder if she'd fallen asleep, then she turned in the darkness. Her voice was muffled as she said, "I never really knew my mother. She died a month after I was born. She was supposed to start chemo, then found out she was pregnant. She didn't want to put me at risk."

"She loved you."

Her voice trembled. "She died because of me," she said softly. "When I was growing up, my father and Bree were always away on their moneymaking schemes. I was mostly alone in a big house, left with a babysitter who got paid by the hour."

Kasimir's heart ached as he pictured Josie as a

child—even more tenderhearted and vulnerable than she was now—feeling alone, unwanted, unloved.

"And from that moment, even as a kid, I knew what I wanted someday. And it wasn't college. It wasn't even a career."

"What is it?" he said in a low voice.

He heard her shuddering intake of breath.

"I want a home," she whispered. "A family of my own. I want to bake pies and do piles of laundry and weed our garden behind the white picket fence. I want an honest, strong husband who will never lie to me, ever, and who will play with our kids and mow our lawn on Saturdays. I want a man I can trust with my heart. A man I can love for the rest of my life." She stopped.

Kasimir's heart lurched violently in his chest. For a moment, he couldn't speak.

"See?" she said in a voice edged with tears. "I told you it was stupid."

He exhaled.

"It's not stupid," he said tightly. For a moment, he closed his eyes. Then he slowly turned to face her in the darkness. His vision adjusted enough to see her eyes glimmer with tears in the shadows of the bed.

I want an honest, strong husband who will never lie to me. A man I can trust with my heart.

Kasimir suddenly envied him, Josie's future husband, whoever he might be. He would deserve her, give her children, provide for her. And she would love him for the rest of her life. Because she had that kind of loyalty. The kind of heart that could love forever.

The irony almost made him laugh. Kasimir envied her next husband. Because even though he was married to her now, Kasimir couldn't be that man. He wasn't her partner, or even her lover. Not even, really, her friend.

But he could be.

"After I pay you for the land," he said, "you and your sister will be free of those old debts. You'll be able to pursue your dreams." He ignored the lump in his throat. "Whatever they might be."

"You're going to pay me?" she gasped. "I thought our deal was just a direct trade—the land for my sister."

"And I always intended to pay you full market value," he lied.

He heard her intake of breath. "Really?" she said wistfully.

No. He'd pay her double the market value. "Yes."

"You don't know what this means to me," she choked out. "We won't have to hide from those men anymore. We'll be free. And if there's any money left after the debts, Bree could use it to start her bed and breakfast."

"Is that what will make you happy?" he said. "Using the money so your sister can fulfill her dreams?"

"Yes!" she cried. "Oh, Kasimir..." He felt her

hand against his rough, unshaven cheek, turning him towards her. He saw the tearful glitter of her eyes. "Thank you. You are—you are…"

With a joyful sob, she threw her arms around him.

Kasimir's arms slowly wrapped around her as her silken negligee slid against the bare skin of his chest. Their bodies pressed together in the bed, and as he felt her soft body against his own, he became all jumbled inside, twisted up and down and turned around.

He put his hand against her cheek. "Josie…" he said hoarsely.

In the shadowy tent, beneath the covers of the bed, he could see her beautiful eyes. He could barely hear her ragged breathing over the pounding of his own heart.

Her skin felt so soft beneath his fingertips. Her arms were bare and wrapped around his naked back. Their faces were inches apart. He wanted to kiss her, hot and hard and deep. He wanted to take her and let his promises fade like mist into the night.

Using every bit of willpower he possessed, he dropped his hand. He pulled away, rolling to the farthest edge of his bed.

"Good night," he choked out.

Silence fell. Then she said softly behind him, "Good night."

Kasimir heard her move to the other side of the bed. He exhaled, closing his eyes. He could still see her beautiful, innocent face, her curvaceous body sheathed in diaphanous silk, shimmering like waves in the flickering light.

He listened to the wind blowing against the tent, the distant whinny of horses, the call of servants' voices across the encampment. And he still heard Josie's voice, sweet and innocent, filled with the trembling edge between desire and fear.

But what if I touch you? she'd asked.

Kasimir didn't have to touch her to feel her. Lying next to her in the soft bed, with blankets warming them in the cool, arid night, there was a desert of empty space between them, but her slightest tremble was an earthquake.

In just a few weeks, once her land was his, Kasimir would trade her for what he wanted most. He would seize control of Xendzov Mining. He'd get justice against those who'd wronged him. He'd finally win.

He should be glad. Excited. His teeth should have been sharpening with anticipation.

But as he listened to Josie's soft, even breathing, all he could think about was what he would soon lose.

He glanced over at her in the darkness. She didn't care about vengeance or money. She wanted to give away her fortune to make her sister happy. She gave everything she had, without worrying if she'd get anything back in return. She didn't even try to protect her heart.

Thank you, Kasimir. He remembered the joy in her voice when she'd thrown her arms around him. *You are...you are...*

He was a selfish bastard with a jet-black heart. He'd kissed her, kidnapped her, kept her prisoner, but she kept forgiving him, again and again.

Rolling onto his back, Kasimir stared up bleakly at the swoop of the tent's canvas, gray with shadow.

Was there some way to keep her in his life? Some way to bind her to him so thoroughly that she'd have no choice but to forgive him the unforgivable?

Two days later, Josie stared up at him with consternation. "You have to be joking."

"Come on," Kasimir wheedled, holding out his hand beneath the hot afternoon sunshine. "You said you wanted to do it."

Glancing back at the tallest sand dune, she licked her lips. "I said it looked fun in theory."

"You know you want to." Wind ruffled his tousled black hair as he smiled down at her. He was casually dressed, in a well-worn black T-shirt that hugged his muscular chest and large, taut biceps and low-slung jeans on his hips. He looked relaxed and younger than she'd ever seen him. He lifted a dark eyebrow wickedly. "You're not scared, are you?"

Josie licked her lips. When he looked at her with that mischievous smile, he made her want to agree to absolutely anything.

But—this?

Furrowing her brow, she looked behind her. Three young Berber boys, around twelve or thirteen years old, were using brightly colored snowboards to careen down the sand, whooping and hollering in Berber, the primary language of the tribe, but the boys' joyous laughter needed no translation.

Josie and Kasimir had been sitting outside the dining tent, lazily eating an early dinner of grapes, flatbread and lamb kabobs, when the boys had started their raucous race. As Josie sipped mint tea, with Kasimir drinking a glass of Moroccan rosé wine beside her, she'd said dreamily, "I wish I could do what they're doing. Be fearless and free."

To her dismay, Kasimir had immediately stood up, brushing sand off his jeans. "So let's go."

Now, he was looking at her with challenge in his eyes. "I have an extra sandboard. I'll show you how."

She scowled. "You know, saying something looks fun and being brave enough to actually do it, are two totally different things!"

"They shouldn't be."

"It looks dangerous. Bree would never let me do it."

"Another good reason."

Josie stiffened. "I wish you would quit slandering Bree—"

"I don't care about her," he interrupted. "I care about *you*. And what you want. Your sister isn't here to stop you. I'm not going to stop you. You say you want to do it. The only one stopping you is you."

She looked up at the dune. It was very tall and the sand looked very hard. She licked her lips. "What if I fall?"

He lifted an eyebrow. "So what if you do?"

"The kids might laugh, or—" she hesitated "—you might."

"Me?" He stared at her incredulously. "Is that a joke? You'd let fear of my reaction keep you from something you want?" His sensual lips lifted as he shook his head. "That doesn't sound like the Josie I know."

She felt a strange flutter in her heart. Kasimir thought she was brave. He thought she was bold.

And she was, when she was with him. She barely recognized herself anymore as the downtrodden housekeeper she'd been in Hawaii. Tomorrow was New Year's Eve, but for Josie, the New Year—her new life—had already begun.

She'd be able to pay off their debts. She hugged the thought to her heart like a precious gift. They'd be free of the dark cloud of fear that had hung over them for ten years, forcing them to stay under the radar with low-paying, nondescript jobs. Bree would be able to start her business. Josie would never feel like a burden again to anyone.

But it would come at a cost. Josie looked up at Kasimir. He could be a rough man, selfish and unfeeling, and yet beneath it all…he truly was a good man. His generosity would change her life.

But she would never see him again. And that thought was starting to hurt. Because she couldn't kid herself.

She'd stopped thinking of their marriage as a business arrangement long ago.

Yesterday, Kasimir had taught her how to ride a horse. Very patiently, until she lost her fear of the big animals' teeth and sharp hooves, until she started to gain confidence. She was still a little sore from their ride that morning, traveling across the dunes to the nearest village, to bring medicine from Marrakech. As she and Kasimir galloped back together across the desert, his eyes had been as blue and bright as the wide Moroccan sky. She lost a new fragment of her heart every time he looked at her with that brilliant, boyish smile.

Just as he was looking at her now.

"Well?" His hand was still outstretched with utter confidence, as if he knew she would not be able to resist.

"Is it soft? Like powder?"

He laughed. "No. It'll leave bruises."

"Sounds fun," she muttered.

"Do you want to try it or not?"

She swallowed, then looked at the boys zooming down the sand dune at incredible speed, on boards lightly strapped to their feet. Heard their roars of laughter and delight. Maybe it wasn't hard. Maybe it was actually quite easy. All she had to do was make the choice.

Josie's eyes narrowed. She was done being afraid—of anything. Done living a life smaller than her dreams.

Holding her breath, she put her hand in his own.

He pulled her close. "Good," he said in a low voice. "Let's do it. Right now."

His face was inches from her own, and a tremble went through her that had nothing to do with fear. Every time Kasimir looked at her, every time he spoke to her, she felt her heart expand until she felt as if she was flying.

Let's do it. Right now.

His grip on her hand tightened. Then he abruptly turned away, disappearing into a nearby tent. And she exhaled.

It had been torture sleeping next to him the last two nights. She'd been so aware of him beside her, it was a miracle she'd gotten any rest at all. Especially the first night, when they'd been talking so late into the darkness, and he'd told her he meant to pay for her land. She'd been so ecstatic that she'd thrown her arms around him. He'd held her so tightly, his eyes dark on hers, and for one moment, she'd thought, really thought, he might break his promise. And here was the really shocking thing…

She'd *wanted* him to.

Her lips had tingled as she'd waited breathlessly for him to lower his mouth savagely to hers and pull her hard against his body. She'd ached to stroke her hands down his hard, tanned chest, laced with dark hair. She'd yearned to feel his pure heat and fire. Her body still shook with the memory of how she'd wanted it. And looking at him, she'd known he felt the same.

But he'd hadn't touched her.

When he'd abruptly turned away, she'd felt bereft—disappointed. Almost heartbroken.

Which made no sense at all. She admired commitment to promises, didn't she? And while they'd been thrown together in a very intimate way, it wasn't as if they had—or ever would have—a real marriage.

She needed to keep reminding herself of that.

Kasimir returned to the table outside the dining tent. He had two snowboards hefted over his shoulders as if they weighed nothing. "Let's go."

Smiling, and far lighter on her feet, she led the way to the top of the dune.

"Like being faster than me, huh?" he said, quirking his eyebrow.

She grinned. "Absolutely."

"We'll see." He answered her with a wicked smile. "Sit down right here."

Obediently, Josie plunked back on the warm sand in her cotton button-down shirt and soft linen pants. As he knelt on the sand in front of her, in his form-fitting T-shirt and loose cargo shorts, she wondered how brave she could really be. He'd promised not to kiss her.

But there was no rule about her kissing him.

"You're going to love this," he said, pulling off her sandals.

She shivered. His hands brushed against the hollows of her bare feet, and her mouth went dry. "I'm sure," she murmured.

He was inches away from her. She could just lean forward and kiss him. Press her lips against his. Could she do it? Was she brave enough?

Kasimir's blue eyes met hers, and he smiled. She wondered how she'd ever thought him cold in Honolulu. Here, he was warm and bright as the blazing desert sun. "Are you nervous?"

"Yes," she whispered, praying he couldn't guess why.

"Don't be."

She gave a soft laugh. "That's easy for you to say."

He placed her bare feet into the straps attached to the board. Standing up, he grabbed her hands and pulled her upright. Josie swayed a little, getting used to the balance. She hadn't been on a board in a long time. She tested the sand with a slight lean and twist. Without snow boots, the ankle support was nonexistent. Turning corners would be nearly impossible.

Kasimir stepped into his own modified snowboard, and his arm shot out to grab her when she started to tilt. "Ready?"

She felt a flash of dizzying heat with his hand on her arm. "Yes," she breathed. "I just need a second to build my courage."

"So." He gave her a slow-rising grin. "Are you interested in racing me?"

"Racing?" Josie looked dubiously over the edge of the dune. It wasn't as steep as some of the mountains she'd snowboarded in Alaska, but that was ten years ago. To say her skills were rusty was an understatement. And boarding down sand was going to be like sailing down a sheet of ice. "I'm not sure that's a good idea."

"I thought you said you liked being faster than me."

"I do."

"Then racing me should be right up your alley." His masculine grin turned downright cocky. "I'll even give you a head start."

Laughter bubbled up to her lips, barely contained. He clearly believed he would be faster. "Um. Thank you?"

"And if you win, you'll get a prize."

"What do you have in mind?"

"Your own private tent," he said recklessly. "For the rest of the time we're in the Sahara."

Her lips parted. Somehow that prize didn't excite her as much as it once would have. "And what about if you win?"

Kasimir looked down at her, and something in his glance made her hold her breath.

"You'll share my bed," he said softly, "and let me make love to you."

CHAPTER SEVEN

SHARE HIS BED?

Josie's lips parted, her heart beating frantically as she looked up at him.

Let him make love to her?

She'd been trying to build up enough courage to kiss him. What would it be like to have him make love to her?

With a shuddering breath, she looked up at him. "I thought you said our marriage was in n-name only."

"I changed my mind," Kasimir said huskily. "You know I want you. And I've come to enjoy your company. There's no reason we shouldn't be...friends."

"Friends who will divorce in a few weeks."

"We could still see each other." He looked at her. "If you want."

Her lips parted. "If *I* want?"

"I would very much like to still see you, after we are divorced." His blue eyes seared through her soul. "For as long as you are still interested in seeing me."

Josie sucked in her breath. For as long as *she* wished to see him? That would be forever!

She looked back over the edge of the dune. It didn't look so frightening anymore. Not with this new challenge. Not with her very virginity on the line.

But…

What about saving herself for love, for commitment, for a lifetime?

She looked back at him. Was Kasimir the man? Was this the time? Was this how she wanted to remember her first night, for the rest of her life?

Her heart pounded in her throat.

Should she let her husband take her virginity?

"Just so you know," she said hesitantly, "my babysitter taught me to snowboard."

"Even better." He gave her a cheeky grin. "So with your head start, you have pretty good odds."

She couldn't help but smile at his smug masculine confidence. "Bree's the gambler, not me."

He gave her a long look beneath the blazing white sun.

"Are you sure about that?" he said softly.

On the other end of the dune, with a loud shout, the boys pushed off again, going straight down, good-naturedly roughhousing and cutting in front of each other as they skidded down the sand.

Josie closed her eyes, took a deep breath, and made her choice.

"I'll do it."

"Excellent."

His blue eyes were beaming. He clearly expected that this would be no contest and that he would easily overtake her. He didn't know that the entirety of the choice was still hers. Would she let him beat her? Or not?

Before her courage could fail her, she breathed, "Just tell me when to go."

"One...two...three...*go!*"

Hastily, Josie tilted her snowboard and went off the edge, plummeting down the dune. Her body remembered the sport, even though her brain had forgotten, and her board picked up speed. For a glorious instant, she flew, and wild joy filled her heart—joy she hadn't felt for ten years.

Then she remembered: if she won, she would sleep alone.

And if she lost, *he would seduce her.*

Slow down, she ordered her feet, and though they protested, she made them turn, her body leaning to drag the board against sand as hard and glassy as ice. It was hard to slow down, when her body yearned to barrel down the dune, like the reckless child she'd once been.

"You'll never win that way," Kasimir called from the top, sounding amused. "Turn your feet to aim straight down."

Josie choked back a wry laugh. He had no idea how hard she was trying *not* to do that. A bead of sweat formed on her forehead from the effort of fighting her body's desire to aim the snowboard straight down and plummet at the speed of flight. Couldn't he tell? Couldn't he see she was actually forcing herself *not* to win?

"Ready or not…"

Behind her, he pushed off the top of the dune. Smiling, she looked up at him as he glided past her on his snowboard. She saw the joy in his face—the same as when they'd galloped together across the desert that morning.

"You are mine now, *kroshka!*" he shouted, and flew past her.

Let me fly fast, half her heart begged.

Let him seduce you, the other half cried.

Then Josie turned her head when she heard a scream at the bottom of the hill. One of the rough-housing boys had lost control and crashed into the other, sending the smaller one skidding down the hard sand in panicked yells. The smaller boy, per-haps twelve years old, had a streak of blood across his tanned face and a trail of red followed him across the pale sand.

Josie didn't think, she just acted. Her knees turned, she leaned forward and she flew down the hill. She had a single glimpse of Kasimir's shocked face as she flew right past him. But she didn't think about that, or anything but the boy's face—the boy who moments before had seemed like a reckless, rambunctious teenager, but who now she saw was barely more than a child.

She reached the bottom of the dune in seconds. Ten feet away from the boy, she twisted hard on her snowboard, digging in for a sharp stop, causing sand to scatter in a wide fan around the boy's friends, who were struggling up towards him. Josie kicked off her snowboard in a single fluid movement and leapt barefoot across the hot sand.

"Are you all right?" she said to the boy in English. His black eyes were anguished, and he answered in sobbing words she didn't understand.

Then she saw his leg.

Beneath the boy's white pants, now covered with blood, she saw the freakish-looking angle of his shin.

She blinked, feeling as though she was going to faint. Careful not to look back at his leg, she reached her arm around the boy's shoulders. "It'll be all right," she whispered, forcing her voice to offer comfort and reassurance. "It'll be all right."

"It's a compound fracture," Kasimir said behind her. She turned and got one vision of his strangely calm face, before he twisted around and spoke sharply in Berber to the other two boys. They scattered, shouting as they ran for the encampment.

Kasimir knelt in the sand beside her. He looked down at the injury. As Josie cuddled the crying boy, Kasimir spoke to him with incredible gentleness in his voice. The boy answered him with a sob.

Carefully, Kasimir ripped the fabric up to the knee to get a closer look at the break. Tearing off a corner of his own shirt, he pushed it into Josie's hand. "Press this just below the knee to slow down the blood."

His voice was calm. Clearly he was good in a crisis. She was not. She swallowed, feeling wobbly. "I can't—"

"You can."

He had such faith in her. She couldn't let him down. Still feeling a bit green, she took a deep breath and pressed the cloth to a point above the wound as firmly as she could.

Rising to his feet, Kasimir crossed back across the sand and returned a moment later with his snowboard. Turning it over to the flat side, he dug sand out from beneath the boy and gently nudged the board beneath the injured leg. He ripped more long bits of fabric from his shirt, giving Josie a flash of his hard, taut abs before he bent to use the board as a splint.

The boy's parents arrived at a run, his mother crying, his father looking blank with fear as he reached out to hold his son's hand. Behind them another man, dark-skinned, with an indigo-colored turban, gave quick brusque orders that all of them obeyed, including Kasimir. Five minutes later, they were lifting the boy onto a makeshift stretcher.

Josie's knees shook beneath her as she started to follow. Kasimir stopped her.

"Go back to the tent," he said. "There's nothing

more you can do." His lips twitched. "Can't have you fainting on us."

She swallowed, remembering how she'd nearly fainted at the sight of the boy's injury. "But I want to help—"

"You have," he said softly. He glanced behind him. "Ahmed's uncle is a doctor. He will take good care of him until the helicopter arrives." He pushed her gently in the other direction. "He'll be all right. Go back to the tent. And pack."

Josie watched anxiously as the boy was carried to the other side of the encampment. He disappeared into a tent, with Kasimir and the others beside him, and she finally turned away. Dazed, she looked down at her clenched hands and saw they were covered in blood.

Slowly, she walked back to the tent she shared with Kasimir. She went to the basin of water and used rose-scented soap to wash the blood off her hands. Drying her hands on a towel, she sank to the bed.

Go back to the tent. And pack.

She gasped as the meaning of those words sank in. She covered her mouth with her hand.

She'd won. By pure mischance, she'd won their race.

There would be no seduction. Instead, from this night forward, she'd be sleeping alone in a separate tent.

Once, Josie would have been relieved.

But now...

Numbly, she rose from their bed. Grabbing her backpack, she started to gather her clothes. Then she stopped, looking around the tent. Kasimir always dumped everything on the floor, in that careless masculine way, knowing it was someone else's job to follow after him and tidy up. Looking across the luxurious carpets piled thickly across the sand, Josie's eyes could see the entirety of her husband's day: the empty water bucket of solid silver. The hand-crafted sandalwood soap. His crumpled pajama pants. And in a corner, his black leather briefcase, so stuffed with papers that it could no longer be closed, none of which he'd glanced at even once since the day they'd arrived here.

In the distance, she heard a sound like rolling thunder.

Tears rose to her eyes, and she wiped them away fiercely. She didn't want to leave him. This was the place where they whispered secrets to each other in the middle of the night. The bed where, if she woke up in the middle of the night, she'd hear the soft sound of his breathing and go back to sleep, comforted that he was beside her.

No more.

When she was finished packing, she grabbed her mother's tattered copy of *North and South*. For the next hour as she waited, sitting on the bed, Josie tried to concentrate on the love story, though she found herself reading the same paragraph over and over.

Kasimir's footstep was heavy as he pushed aside the heavy cotton flap of the door. She looked up from her book, her heart fluttering, as it always did at the breathtaking masculine beauty of his face, the hard edge of his jawline, dark with five o'clock shadow, and the curved edge of his cheekbones. His blue eyes looked tired.

Setting down the book on the bed, Josie asked anxiously, "Is he going to be all right?"

"Yes." He went to the basin and poured clear, fresh water over his dirty hands. "His uncle put a proper splint on his leg. The helicopter just left to take them all to the hospital in Marrakech."

"Thank heaven," Josie whispered.

Kasimir didn't answer. But as he dried his hands, she saw the shadows beneath his eyes, the tightness of his shoulders.

Without a word, she came up behind him. Closing her eyes, she wrapped her arms around his body, pressing her cheek against his back until she felt his tension slowly relax into her embrace.

A moment later, with a shudder, he finally turned around in her arms to face her.

"You were the first to reach him," he said in a low voice. "Thank you."

Her eyes glistened with tears. "It was nothing."

Kasimir gave her a ghost of a smile. "You were much faster than I thought."

"I told you my father and Bree were gone a lot," she said in a small voice. "My babysitter was a former championship snowboarder from the Lower Forty-Eight."

"You grew up in Anchorage, didn't you?" He gave a low, humorless laugh. "Had a season pass at Alyeska?"

"Since I was four years old." She gave him a trembling smile. "If it's any consolation, I'm faster than Bree, too. She's horrible on the mountain. Strap skis or a snowboard on her feet and she'll plow nose-first into the snow."

"I'll keep that in mind."

"But you and I," she said quickly, "it was a close race…"

"Not even." He bared his teeth in a smile. "You won by a mile."

With an intake of breath, Josie searched his gaze. "Kasimir, you have to know that I never meant to—"

"And I see you've packed. Good." He glanced down at her backpack. "I'll show you to your new tent."

"Fantastic," she said, crestfallen. Against her will, she hungrily searched his handsome face, his deep blue eyes, his sensual lips. She didn't want to be away from him. *She didn't.* "If not for the accident," she said, glancing at him sideways, "the race could have ended very differently…"

"Josie, please," Kasimir growled. "Do not attempt

to assuage my masculine pride. That would just add insult to injury." Picking up her backpack, he tossed it over his shoulder. "I'll send over your trunk of new clothes later. You'll likely only be here at the camp for another week or two."

"Just me? Not you?"

He set his jaw. "I'm going to go look for your sister."

"I thought you said it was too soon," Josie said faintly.

He gave her a smile that didn't quite reach his eyes. "I'll leave you and go get her. Both the things you wanted. It's your lucky day."

It was ending. He was leaving her. She thought of the time she'd wasted, longing for him to kiss her and doing nothing. Waiting—always waiting—with a timid heart!

"But you said you couldn't trust me. That if you brought back my sister early, I might demand a hundred million dollars for my land..."

He gave a hard laugh. "You're more trustworthy than anyone in this crazy, savage world. Including me." Grabbing her upper arms, he looked down at her. "Serves me right," he muttered. "I never should have tried to get around my promise."

"Take me with you."

His eyes widened, then he slowly shook his head. "It'll be better...for your sake...for both of us...it's best that we separate."

"Separate," she echoed, feeling hollow.

"Until the land comes through."

She swallowed. "Until we divorce."

His lips curved into a humorless smile. "You know what, I'm almost glad I lost." He tucked a loose tendril of her brown hair behind her ear, then looked straight into her eyes. "Save yourself, Josie. For your next husband. For a man who can deserve you. Who can love you," he added softly.

Turning away, Kasimir started to walk towards the door.

"I intended to lose the race," she blurted out.

She heard his intake of breath. He slowly turned to face her.

"Why?" he asked in a low voice.

She gulped. She had to be brave. To tell the truth. And do it now. Now, without thinking about the risk or cost. Now.

Josie crossed the tent to him. Standing up on her tiptoes, she put her hands on his shoulders and looked straight into his startled blue eyes. "Because I wanted you to seduce me," she whispered.

And leaning forward, she kissed his lips.

So much for his brilliant intelligence. Kasimir had thought he was so smart, finding a loophole around his promise. Passing her in their race down the dune, he'd felt triumphant, his body tight, knowing he all but had her in his arms.

Then there was a scream, and she'd flown past him. She was such an accomplished snowboarder that she'd had no problem handling the textural differences between snow and sand. And she'd seen the source of the scream, the injured boy, half a second faster than he had. It was enough to make any man feel slow. Stupid and slow.

Which was exactly how Kasimir had felt pacing the tent of the boy's family as his uncle, a doctor trained in Marrakech, worked on the boy's ugly compound fracture with his limited instruments at hand. Kasimir had looked down at the sobbing boy, wishing he could do more than order a helicopter on his satellite phone, wishing they didn't have to wait so long, and most of all, dreading the long, jarring journey the boy would face traveling to the hospital in Marrakech.

After Ahmed was loaded on the helicopter with a stretcher, Kasimir had evaded the tearful thanks of Ahmed's family. Shoulders tight, he returned to the tent where Josie waited—not for his seduction, but for her freedom.

The whole afternoon, from start to finish, had left the acrid sourness of failure in his mouth.

And then—Kasimir had tasted the sweetness of Josie's lips against his.

She'd reached her hands around his shoulders, lifting up on her tiptoes, and he'd just stared down at her in shock, telling himself he was completely misreading the situation. Josie, the inexperienced virgin, wouldn't make the first move.

Why would she kiss him? He was a man who

stood for nothing and no one. She was an angel who knew how to fly.

I intended to lose the race. Because I wanted you to seduce me.

He heard a soft sigh from the back of her throat. Saw her close her eyes. And she pressed her soft, trembling lips to his.

He didn't immediately respond. He was too amazed. But when she grew shy, and started to draw away, a growl came from the back of his throat. Closing his eyes, he roughly pulled her back against his body and returned her kiss with force, with all the passion and longing he'd tried so hard not to feel. He let himself feel it—all of it—and desire overwhelmed him as it never had before.

Her lips parted as he deepened the kiss. She returned his embrace awkwardly, hungrily. And it was the best kiss of his life.

Outside the tent, he heard the rising wind flapping and rattling against the heavy waxed canvas. But he was lost in her. Her lips were so soft, her body so womanly, her soul so pure. As he ran his hands down her back, over her loose cotton shirt, he felt the press of her breasts against his muscled chest. Her brown hair now tumbled down her back in waves, tangling in his fingers.

It could have been hours or even days that he kissed her, standing with her in his arms, holding her body tightly against his own. He flicked her mouth lightly with his tongue, guiding her lips, teaching her to kiss. His tongue brushed against hers, luring her to explore further. With a sigh of pleasure, she leaned towards him, her arms tightening around his shoulders.

Josie. So reckless. So beautiful. She had such strange power. She made him want things he shouldn't want…. Made him feel things he didn't know he could still feel….

Lifting her into his arms, never ending their kiss, he carried her to the four-poster bed he'd shared with her in painful chastity for two nights. As he laid her back against the mattress, he looked down at her beautiful face.

"Tell me you don't want me," he said hoarsely. "Tell me to leave you be."

He held his breath, as if waiting for a verdict of his life or death. She shook her head slightly. His heart twisted.

Then her full, pink lips lifted into a tender smile. Her brown eyes shimmered, glowing with desire, and she reached up for him, pulling him down against her in clear answer.

He felt her body beneath him, and knew he'd never again suffer the agony of sleeping beside her without being able to touch her. Because nothing on earth would stop him from taking her now.

Cupping her face, he kissed her passionately, stretching her back against the bed. His hands moved up and down her body until he finally reached beneath her cotton shirt. He felt her trembling hands stroke his bare chest beneath his own ripped shirt, torn into bandages on the dune. Her satin-soft fingertips ran along his flat belly and bare chest, and he gasped at the amazing sensation. He kissed down her throat, and his fingers were suddenly clumsy as he tried to unbutton her shirt, finally popping off the buttons in his desperation to feel the warmth of her skin against his own.

Yanking her shirt off her body, he threw it to the carpet and was mesmerized by full breasts barely contained within a lacy black bra. He sucked in his breath. Distracted, he didn't notice her tugging on his T-shirt until suddenly it was pulled off over his head. He felt the exploratory touch of her fingertips over his flat nipples and down the light dusting of black hair that pointed like an arrow down his muscled body.

Josie. Was this really going to happen? His heart was in his throat as he looked down at her. Here, now?

Outside, the hot wind howled against the tent as he kissed her deeply, pushing her down beneath him, against the soft pillows. He cupped his hands over her bra, feeling the weight of her breasts beneath his hands. He pushed her legs apart with his knee, grinding himself slowly against her, with only fabric separating them. She trembled as he liberated one large breast completely from the bra, watching the rosy nipple pucker and harden beneath the warmth of his breath before he suckled her.

In a single movement, he unclasped the bra and tossed it aside. Leaning back over her, he felt her shiver as he slowly kissed down her neck. Pressing her full breasts together, he kissed the crevice between them, licking her skin.

He felt her fingers tangle in his dark hair as she gasped, clutching him to her. He kissed down to the soft curve of her belly, feeling her tremble, feeling the damp heat of her skin. He slowly pulled off her linen pants, lingering against her thighs and the secret hollow beneath her knees. He removed his cargo shorts. Wearing only his silk boxers, which at the moment were uncomfortably tight, he slid his hips between her legs. Instinctively, she swayed as he rocked himself against her, back and forth over her lacy black panties. He heard her intake of breath as her hands clutched his shoulders, holding him against her.

His lips lowered to suckle a full, pink nipple. He lightly squeezed her breast, pushing her nipple more deeply into his mouth. He heard her soft muffled gasp as he ran his tongue in a swirling motion, nibbling and sucking, as his hand toyed with the other nipple. And all the while, he was slowly grinding himself against her, with only the thin separation of silk between them.

Her hands suddenly gripped his hair. "Stop."

Kasimir sucked in his breath as he pulled back. His body ached as he held himself in check, looking down at her. It would kill him, but if she wanted him to stop....

Josie reached up, running her hands down his bare chest, to the edge of his silk boxers. She looked up, her cheeks red, her eyes bright. "I want to see you. To touch you."

He exhaled.

"Yes."

With tantalizing slowness, she ran her hands along the edge of the waistband, and then—*and then*—he held his breath as she reached beneath the silk. She stroked the hardness of his shaft, running her fingers along the ridges and tip.

He heard a low hoarse gasp, and realized it was his own. Her eyes were huge as they met his. And then...

She suddenly smiled.

It was a smug, feminine smile, full of infinite mystery and pride—as if she'd realized the depths of power she held over him, as she held him completely in her hands.

She pulled down the silk, revealing his body completely to her gaze. She ran her hand over him, exploring. His breathing became ragged. He closed his eyes. Her slightest touch made him wild. He felt as though he could explode at any moment...

No. His eyes flew open, narrowed. With a growl, he pushed her back against the bed. Pulling at her panties, he tugged them slowly down her legs and tossed them to the carpeted sand. He stroked her calves, her knees, then moved back upward, to her thighs. Gently, he pushed her legs apart.

He felt her tremble at being so exposed. She tried to close her knees.

"What are you doing?" she breathed.

"Surrender to me," he whispered. And he lowered his head.

First, he kissed her inner thighs. Then he moved higher. Holding her against the mattress, he stretched her legs wide. For a moment, he just allowed her to feel the warmth and sensation of his breath. Then, very slowly, he moved his kisses to the core of her pleasure. She abruptly stopped struggling.

He took a long, delicious taste. "Like honey," he murmured.

She gave a soft gasp beneath him. He licked her again, swirling his tongue lightly against her, then widening his tongue fully. He pushed a single thick fingertip an inch into her tight, wet core.

She cried out, writhing beneath him as she gripped the sheets. Licking her, sucking her hard nub, he thrust a second finger inside her gently, and she moved her hips unthinkingly, twisting in an agony of need. He lapped her with his tongue, swirling against her taut center, as he felt her tense up. Her back arched off the bed, higher, higher still, until she exploded with a scream of joy.

And just in time. His whole body was sweaty and aching from holding himself back. As she exploded in her pleasure, he could no longer wait. In a swift mindless movement, he drew back and positioned himself between her legs. Lowering his head, he kissed her mouth, and then thrust himself roughly inside her, sheathing himself deep, deep, deep.

CHAPTER EIGHT

JOSIE GASPED AGAINST his lips as he thrust inside her, and she felt an unexpected fleeting pain.

Still deep inside her, he did not move, allowing her to gently stretch to accommodate him. His mouth was motionless against hers in a suspended kiss as she grew accustomed to the now dulling pain. She barely heard the wind outside, or felt the soft mattress beneath her and the weight of him over her. She was overwhelmed by the huge feel of him inside her.

Then, keeping his body still, he flicked his tongue against hers, tantalizing her with a hot, seductive kiss as she grew accustomed to the thick feel of him, like silk and steel inside her. The pain receded, like a wave drawing back beneath her feet. He pressed his naked body over hers, cupping her face with one hand to kiss her more deeply, and her hand trailed down his shoulder to his back as pleasure began to build anew inside her.

She'd never known the pain would be so great— and yet so suddenly gone. She'd never known pleasure could be so intense, so explosive—and could just as suddenly begin again. Sex was a more intense experience than she'd ever imagined. It left her breathless and weak.

So did he.

Josie's heart raced, pounding frantically in her throat, as she looked up at his handsome, sensual face. She'd been bold and daring enough to tell him the truth, and this was her reward. *This.*

Their hot, naked bodies twisted and moved together, sweaty, hard, sliding. She ran her hands down his chest, feeling his hard muscles and taut hollows. His body felt as amazing as it looked. Pulling him down against her, she kissed his shoulder, tasting and nibbling the salt of his skin.

With a shudder, Kasimir pushed her back against the bed, kissing down her throat. She gasped, tilting her head.

He finally began to move inside her, riding her. He filled her in a way she'd never imagined, deeper with each thrust. Her hands scratched slowly down his back, finally clutching his hard backside. She felt new tension inside her, coiled to spring. She felt the tautness of his muscles, heard the hoarse pant of his breath, and knew he was fighting to keep his body under control.

And *she* was causing that. She was the one driving him wild with desire. Her. Plain, frumpy Josie.

But she wasn't that Josie anymore. He'd changed her. Or she'd changed herself. But either way, she'd become the woman she'd always known she was born to be. Brave. Reckless. Even a little wicked...

His eyes closed. His sensual lips parted in a silent gasp as he pushed inside her, filling her to the hilt, stretching her to the breaking point. He was trying not to hurt her, she realized. He was still holding himself back.

Reaching her arms around his shoulders, she dug her fingernails into his flesh and whispered, "Don't be afraid."

His eyes flew open. He looked down at her with a choked intake of breath.

Giving him a little smile, she ran her hand softly down his hard, muscular body. "Stop holding back."

A growl came from the back of his throat, ending in a hiss. Pushing her back hard against the bed, he pushed more roughly inside her, riding her faster and deeper.

Now it was deepening pleasure. Their intertwined bodies tangled in desperate passion, clutching each other tightly as her hips lifted to meet each explosive thrust. Josie heard the hot wind howling outside and didn't care if a sandstorm flung the tent up into the sky. She was already flying....

The new pleasure continued to soar, rising and surpassing the first. It was deeper and different and sharper than before. Clutching his shoulders, she hung on for dear life as the pleasure grew so big it was almost too much to bear. Finally, it exploded inside her. Sucking in her breath, she tossed back her head and screamed with joy, heedless of who might hear, as she fell, fell, fell, plummeting off the edge of reason.

In that same instant, she heard his low answering roar. He slammed inside her with one final deep thrust, gripping her tightly with a low hoarse shout.

His muscular, sweaty body was heavy as he collapsed on top of her. Rolling next to her on the bed, he clutched her to his heart. A smile traced Josie's lips as she closed her eyes, pressing her cheek against his chest. She felt changed, reborn in his arms. She'd been born to be his wife….

It could have been minutes later, or hours, when Josie's eyes flew open in the darkness. She realized she hadn't just given her virginity to Kasimir tonight.

She'd given him her heart.

So this was how it was to fall in love. In all the books she'd read, all the movies she'd seen, she'd dreamed and wondered how it would be. What it would feel like, when she gave herself to a man completely.

It was like this. Overwhelming. Powerful. Sweet and full of longing. But also…

Terrifying.

Because loving him was an astoundingly simple thing to do. She'd been dazzled by him from the moment they'd met. Infatuated before they were wed. But now…she was in love. Truly and deeply in love for the first time.

Josie swallowed, slowly turning to look at the handsome face of the man sleeping beside her. One side of his face was turned toward the silver moonlight glowing softly through the white canvas. The other side of his face was in shadow, dark and harsh.

And that was Kasimir's soul. This was the man she'd given herself to—body and heart. The man she loved had one side filled with light. This side encouraged, protected, demanded, respected. He was strong and calm in a crisis; he'd rushed to the side of the injured boy.

But Kasimir's other half...was filled with darkness.

There are rumors about me, he'd said. *That I am more than ruthless. That I am half-insane, driven mad by my hunger for revenge.*

But loving him changed everything. She no longer wished to escape him. Or even to be his make-believe wife for a few weeks in a marriage of convenience.

Josie wanted to be his real wife. Always and forever. Complete with children and the white picket fence.

But Prince Kasimir Xendzov was not a white-picket-fence kind of man.

She turned her head, blinking back tears. Such a risk. Such a stupid risk. She loved the good in him—the man he'd once been, the man he could be again.

But the pain of past betrayals had warped his

soul, turning him dark and ruthless. Giving him reason to keep the world at a distance. Her heart twisted in her chest.

Could she make him see that forgiving his brother wouldn't be weakness, but strength—freeing him for a new life? Could she show him that the world could be so much more? She yearned to show him his life, his future, had just begun.

Just as hers had…

With a low sigh, she nestled closer to him in bed. His eyes remained closed, but his strong arms instinctively pulled her closer against the warmth of his body.

It felt so protective, so good. Closing her eyes, she pressed her cheek against his chest.

She would find a way. She yawned, safe and sleepy in his arms. Kasimir had changed her life.

For so long, Josie had been afraid. Since she was twelve, Bree had protected her like a mother hen, not letting her take risks, warning her about the evils of the world. Josie had listened. After all, Bree, older by six years, was the smart one. The strong one. Josie was the burden. The helpless, hapless one. The one who, just by being born, had caused her mother to die. What right did Josie have to ask for anything at all? What right to speak her mind, to make a fuss, to live her dreams?

But Kasimir had changed her, completely and irrevocably. He'd forced her to be who she really was inside. And shown her that living boldly was the only way to honor the sacrifice her mother had made, and the life she'd been given.

He'd done that for her. She yearned to do something for him. She wanted to teach him that being vulnerable, that trusting others, could be his greatest strength. Josie snuggled deeper into his arms. She would help him break free from the chains of anger and revenge....

Morning sunlight was bright against the white canvas of the tent when Josie opened her eyes. She sat up abruptly. She was alone amid the tangled sheets of the bed. Much of the tent, too, was empty. She saw his packed suitcase beside her own backpack at the door. Weird. Were they going somewhere?

But where was Kasimir?

Kasimir. Just his name was like a song in her heart. Rising from the bed, she splashed fresh cool water on her face from the basin, then pulled on a clean T-shirt, a cotton skirt and sandals from the wardrobe and went outside.

Her heart pounded as she looked for him. She was going to tell him she loved him. Now. Today. The instant she saw him.

But where was he? All of the servants in the encampment seemed to be rushing around strangely, boxing up, packing. She wondered if they were tidying up from the wind storm the night before. Maybe it had been a big one. Not that Josie had noticed. She'd been too distracted by the sensual storm in their bed. A sweet smile lifted her lips. She started towards one of the women, to ask if she'd seen Kasimir. Then Josie stopped.

He was standing alone on the highest dune. His powerful dark silhouette dazzled her. He was like the sun—her northern star.

With an intake of breath, she climbed the sand dune towards him, as fast as she could go. Looking around, she realized she'd come to love the vastness and beauty of the desert. It didn't feel so lonely anymore, or make her feel small.

As long as she was with Kasimir, the world was a wondrous place.

She stopped. Was she making a mistake to tell him she loved him? Would it ruin everything?

She looked at him again, and her shoulders relaxed. Her momentary fear floated away, evaporating like dark smoke into the blue sky, like a shadow beneath the bright Moroccan sun. She didn't have to be afraid. Not anymore. Kasimir had believed in her.

And now, she believed in herself.

"I'm not afraid," she said aloud. Her legs regained their strength. She started to walk towards his broad-shouldered shadow on the top of the dune, silhouetted against the bright sun.

A warm desert wind blew against her skin, tossing tendrils of her hair in her face as she reached him. She was so happy to see his handsome face that tears filled her eyes. "Kasimir. There's something I need to…"

"I have good news," he interrupted coldly.

She looked at him more closely. His desert garb was gone. No more tight black T-shirts. No more cargo shorts or jeans, either. Instead, he was back in his dark suit with a tie and vest. He looked exactly like the same dangerous tycoon she'd first met in Honolulu.

In the distance, she heard a loud buzzing noise. Suddenly feeling uncertain, she echoed, "Good news?"

He gave a single sharp nod. "I'm taking you with me. To Russia. So I can get your sister."

"Oh," Josie said faintly. "That is good news."

It was. But why was his handsome face so expressionless, as if they were total strangers? Why did he seem so suddenly distant, as if they hadn't spent last night ripping off each other's clothes? Why did he look at her as if he barely knew her when just hours before he had been gasping with sweaty pleasure, deep inside her?

"Time to go," he said flatly.

Looking at him in his suit, Josie suddenly felt cold in the warm morning air. The joyful, emotional barbarian with the unguarded heart, the one who'd taught her to ride horses, to snowboard sand, to make love—was gone. She bit her lip. "When?"

He glanced behind him, and she saw an approaching helicopter in the wide blue sky. "Right now."

Shivering, she wrapped her arms around her body, feeling chilly in her cotton shirt. They stood only a few feet apart on the sand, but there was suddenly a deep, wide ocean between them that she didn't understand.

His cruel, sensual lips curved. "We're leaving to find your sister. Aren't you happy?"

"I am," she said miserably. Then, reminding herself she was brave and bold, she lifted her gaze. "But why are you acting like this?"

He blinked. "Like what?"

"Like…" She looked straight into his eyes. "Like last night meant nothing."

"It meant something." He took a step towards her, his face hard as a marble statue. "It meant…a few hours of fun."

It was like a stab in the heart. "Fun?"

Kasimir gave her a coldly charming smile, looking every inch the heartless playboy the world believed him to be. "Oh, yes." He tilted his head, looking at her sideways. "Definitely fun."

For an instant, Josie could hardly breathe through the pain. Then she saw a flash of something in his expression, something quickly veiled and hidden. Her eyes widened as she searched his gaze.

"You're deliberately pushing me away," she breathed.

His expression hardened as he set his jaw. "Don't."

"Last night meant something to you. I know it did!"

"It was an amusement, just to pass the time. But that time is over. Let's get this done. Get our divorce. Then we'll never have to see each other again."

She licked her lips as the approaching helicopter grew louder. "But you said...we could still be friends...."

"Friends?" He gave a harsh, ugly laugh. "You really think that would work? You expect me to give up my life and join you in your fairy-tale world, where families love and forgive?" He slowly walked around her, his eyes glittering in the white sun. "Tell me. Are you already picturing me mowing the lawn outside your storybook cottage with the white picket fence?"

"You're using my dreams against me?" she whispered. His sneer ripped through her heart. She blinked back tears. "Why are you being so cruel?"

Kasimir stopped. The helicopter landed on the pad some distance behind him, causing sand to fly in waves. His black hair whipped wildly around his face as he looked down at her. When he finally spoke, his voice had changed.

"Whatever happened between us last night," he said quietly, "cannot last. Someday soon you will learn the truth about me. And you will hate me."

She shook her head fiercely. "I will never—"

"I'm not giving up my revenge." His blue eyes suddenly blazed. Reaching out, he grabbed her shoulders. "Don't you understand? You can't make me give it up, no matter how good or kind you are, or how you look at me. I'm never going to change, so don't even try."

"But you can," she choked out. A single tear spilled over her lashes. "You could be so much more…."

A flash of raw vulnerability filled his stark blue eyes as he stared down at her. "A woman like you would be a fool to care about a man like me," he said in a low voice. "Don't do it, Josie. Don't."

She stared at him with an intake of breath.

"It is growing late." The cold mask reasserted itself on his handsome face. Abruptly releasing her, he turned towards the waiting helicopter. "Time to go."

An ache filled her throat.

"It's too late already," she whispered, but he'd already turned away.

CHAPTER NINE

HAPPINESS COULD BE corrosive as acid, when you knew it wasn't going to last.

Kasimir gripped the phone to his ear as he stared at the snowy Russian forest outside the window of the dark-walled study. Greg Hudson's voice was grating on the other end of the line.

"So—the New Year's Eve ball tonight? I am tired of waiting," the man complained.

"Yes. And once you are paid," Kasimir replied tightly, "you will never contact me again, or speak of our deal to anyone."

"Of course, of course. I just want the money you owe me. Especially since my boss at the Hale Ka'nani found out about your bribe and fired me."

"You are sure Vladimir and Bree are attending the ball?"

"Yes. I've been watching them, as you said. You owe me extra, for freezing my butt off in Russia. I could be sipping piña coladas on a beach right now."

"Eleven o'clock." Kasimir tossed his phone across the desk. With a deep breath, he looked back out the window. It was the first time he'd seen snow in ten years.

And a million miles from where he'd woken up that morning. In the heat of the Sahara, waking in Josie's arms to the soft pink dawn, Kasimir had known perfect happiness for the first time in his adult life. He'd held her, listening to the soft sound of her breath as she slept. For thirty seconds, he'd known peace. He'd known joy. And the feelings were alien and terrifying....

Then he'd known that it would all soon end.

So let it end, he thought grimly. After returning to Marrakech, and a stop for the necessary travel documents, he'd taken Josie to Russia in his private jet, to this small remote dacha—a luxurious cabin in the forest outside St. Petersburg.

He'd been cold to her. He'd done what needed to be done. He was hanging on to his control by a thread. He knew what she wanted. He couldn't give in.

He could *not* let himself care for Josie. He couldn't listen to her alluring whispers about a different future. She made him feel things he did not want to feel. Uncertain. Raw. With a heart full of longing for a world that did not, could not exist.

It was time to face reality.

Tonight. New Year's Eve. He would wait until he could speak to Bree Dalton alone, at the exclusive luxury ball at the Tsarina's palace. He would give her his blackmail ultimatum. Now. Before Josie convinced his heart to turn completely soft.

He exhaled.

And once he'd done it…he would tell Josie the truth about who he was. The kind of man who felt nothing, who got what he wanted at any cost. For once and for all, he would wipe that look of adoration off her face. Because he would not, could not give up his plans for revenge. Or keep Josie from finding out about it. For their time together in the Sahara, he'd been happy, truly happy. But it was all about to end.

So let it end. Now. Before the corrosive happiness of caring for Josie, and knowing she'd soon leave, burned his soul straight to ash.

"Kasimir?" Her sweet voice spoke behind him. "Who were you talking to on the phone?"

He whirled around to face her in the dacha's dark study. The decor was very masculine. But then, he'd borrowed this country house from an old acquaintance, Prince Maksim Rostov, who was spending the week of New Year's in California with his wife, Grace, and their two young children.

Kasimir cleared his throat. He kept his voice as cold as he could. "No one that concerns you."

Josie's beautiful eyes filled with hurt. "I thought, now we were in Russia, maybe we could talk…."

"There's nothing to talk about." He told himself he was doing her a favor. This small hurt would be nothing compared to how she'd feel when she discovered he'd kept her prisoner all this time to black-mail her sister.

Let her learn the truth of his dark heart by de-grees.

He had to let her go.

He had to push her away.

Now. Before she made him surrender his very soul.

Kasimir straightened the black tie of his tuxedo. "I have to go."

Her brown eyes were deep with unspoken long-ing. "Go where?"

"Out," he said shortly.

She bit her lip. "In a tuxedo...?"

"Bree and Vladimir will be at the most exclusive New Year's Eve ball in the city. I'm going to go have a little chat." He stopped, then kissed her briefly, not on her lips, but on her forehead. He gave her a smile that didn't meet his eyes. "Your sister will be surprised to hear we're married."

"Take me with you," she said.

He shook his head. "Sorry."

"I need to explain to her why I married you." She swallowed. "She'll be so disappointed in me, that I did it to break my father's trust...."

"Bree? Disappointed in you?" he said harshly. His eyes blazed. "You gave up everything to save her." Forcing his shoulders to relax, he pulled a col-orful, brightly decorated phone out of his pocket. "And you can explain that."

She blinked. "What are you doing with my dead phone?"

"All charged up now. I'll give it to her so she can call you here. Tonight."

Kasimir could see the emotions fighting for domination in her expression. But what she finally said was, "Thanks. That is very—kind…"

Kind. Again. Scowling, he turned away. "I have to go."

"Wait," she choked out.

He stopped at the door. He looked back at her.

Josie's beautiful eyes were huge, her soft cheeks pale. "Just tell me one thing," she whispered. "Do you—do you regret taking me to bed last night?"

His eyes met hers.

"Yes," Kasimir said simply, and as he saw her face crumple, he knew it was true. He regretted that for the rest of his life, he'd be haunted by the memory of a perfect woman he could never deserve. A woman he could never have again. A woman who would despise him forever the instant she heard he'd blackmailed her sister.

"Oh." It was the kind of gasp a person makes when they'd just been punched in the gut. She blinked fast, fighting back tears. He wanted to comfort her. Instead, he said, "I'll be back after midnight. Don't wait up."

"Happy New Year," she whispered behind him, but he kept walking, straight out of the house.

As his chauffeur drove him away from the dacha,

heading down the lonely road through the snowy forest, Kasimir looked up at the icy moon in the dark sky. His hands tightened in his lap. He missed her. After ten years alone, without ever letting down his guard to another human soul, he missed Josie. He missed his wife.

But his days with her were numbered. They were ticking by with every minute on the clock. And so this had to be done. Although suddenly, even in his mind, he didn't like to specify what *it* was.

It was betraying her.

The New Year's Eve ball was in full swing when he arrived at the elegant palace outside St. Petersburg. Beautiful, glamorously dressed women stared at him hard as he stepped out of the expensive car, and he felt their eyes travel down the length of his tuxedo as they licked their red lips.

In another world, he would have been only too glad to take advantage of the pleasurable services clearly on offer. But not now. Kasimir looked down at the plain gold wedding band on his finger. There was only one woman his body hungered after now. The one woman who would soon leave him, no matter how much he cared. Turning away, he backed into the shadows, avoiding notice as much as he could. Watching. Looking.

"There you are," Greg Hudson said from behind a potted plant. He nodded towards the dance floor. "Your brother and *Bree*," he panted her name, "are over there."

Kasimir's lip curled as he looked from the man's greasy hair to his totally inappropriate sport jacket, which barely covered his pot belly. With distaste, he withdrew an envelope from his pocket.

Hudson's eyes lit up, but as he reached for the envelope, Kasimir grabbed his wrist. "If you even hint to Vladimir I'm here, I will take back every penny, and the rest out of your hide."

"I wouldn't—couldn't—" With a gulp, the man backed away. "So goodbye, then. Um. *Da svedanya.*"

Turning away with narrowed eyes, Kasimir looked out at the dance floor. He moved slowly through the people, on the edge of the party. Then he saw his brother.

Seeing Vladimir's face was almost startling. For a split instant, Kasimir saw him walking ahead in the snow on the way to school, always ahead of him, whether chopping firewood, chasing newborn calves through the Alaskan forest, or fishing frozen lakes for hours through a cut-out hole in the ice. *Wait for me, Volodya,* Kasimir had always cried. *Wait for me.* But his brother had never waited.

Now, Kasimir's jaw set.

In the last ten years, Vladimir had grown more powerful, more distinguished in his appearance and certainly richer. He also now had faint lines at his eyes as he smiled down at the woman in his arms.

Bree Dalton. The older sister that Josie had sacrificed so much, risked so much, to save. And there was Bree, laughing and flirting and apparently having the time of her life in his great-grandmother's peridot necklace and a fancy ball gown.

Watching them with dark thoughts, Kasimir waited in the shadows until Vladimir left Bree alone on the dance floor. And then Kasimir approached her. He talked to her in low, terse tones. And five minutes later, he left Bree on the dance floor, her face shocked and trembling with fear.

Serves her right, Kasimir thought with cold fury as he left the Tsarina's palace. Josie had been so desperate to save her, and Bree had been enjoying herself all this time as Vladimir's mistress. A tight ache filled his throat.

So much for Josie's *sacrifice.*

And still, after everything she'd done for Bree, when Josie had briefly spoken to her sister, she'd still tried to apologize.

Kasimir exhaled as his chauffeur turned the black Rolls-Royce farther from the palace and through the snowy, frozen sprawl of St. Petersburg. Letting the two sisters briefly speak on the phone had been a calculated gamble.

Where are you? Bree had gasped. There was a pause, in which Kasimir overheard Josie's blurted-out apology, begging her sister's forgiveness for her marriage of convenience. Panicked, Bree had cried, *But where are you?*

He'd taken the phone away before Josie could blurt out that she was right here, in St. Petersburg, not in Morocco at all. Now, Kasimir silently looked out at the moonlit night, at passing fields of snow, laced with black trees.

It was just past midnight. A brand-new year. As he traveled out into the countryside, towards the dacha, he should have been feeling triumphant. His brother had no idea he was about to lose his company, his lover, everything.

Bring the signed document to my house in Marrakech within three days, Kasimir had told Bree coldly.

She'd answered, *And if I fail?*

He'd given her a cold smile. *Then you'll never see your sister again. She'll disappear into the Sahara. And be mine. Forever.*

Now, Kasimir clawed back his hair as he stared out the window at the moonlit night, with only the occasional lights of a town to illuminate the Russian land in the darkness.

In seventy-two hours, Bree would meet him in Marrakech and provide him with a contract, unknowingly signed by Vladimir, that would give him complete ownership of Xendzov Mining OAO. He should have been ecstatic.

Instead, he couldn't stop thinking about how Josie had felt, soft and breathless, in his arms all night, as the hot desert wind howled against their tent, and they slept, naked in each other's arms, face-to-face, heart-to-heart. Her reckless, fearless emotion had saturated his body and soul. He couldn't forget the adoration in her eyes last night—and the shocked hurt in them today.

His hands shook at the thought of the conversation he'd soon have with his wife. Looking down, he realized he was twisting the gold ring on his left hand so hard his fingertip had started to turn white. He released the ring, then exhaled, leaning back in the leather seat. The last lights disappeared as they went deeper into the countryside. Dawn was still hours away on the first of January, the darkest of deep Russian winter.

The car finally turned down a quiet country road surrounded by the black, bare trees of a snowy forest. Past the empty guardhouse, the car continued down a road that was bumpy and long. The trees parted and he saw a large Russian country house in pale gray wood, overlooking a dark lake frosted with moonlight.

The limo pulled in front of the house and abruptly stopped. For a moment, he held his breath. The chauffeur opened his door, and Kasimir felt a chilling rush of cold air. Pulling a black overcoat over his tuxedo, he stepped out into the snowy January night.

As he walked towards the front door, the gravel crunched beneath his feet, echoing against the trees. In the pale gleaming lights from the windows, he could see the icicles of his breath.

As the chauffeur drove the car away towards the

distant barn that was used as a garage, Kasimir went to the front door and found it was unlocked.

Surprised, he pushed open the door. He walked into the dark, silent foyer. The house was silent. As the grave.

Where were the bodyguards?

"Hello?" he called harshly. No answer. With a sickening feeling, he suddenly remembered the guardhouse had been empty, as well. With no one minding the door, anyone could have walked right in and found Josie sleeping, helpless and alone.

He sucked in his breath. This was a safe area, but he had plenty of enemies. Starting with his own brother. If somehow—somehow—Vladimir had found out he was here...

"Josie!" he cried. He ran up the stairs three steps at a time. He rushed down the hall to their bedroom. If anything had happened, he would never forgive himself for leaving her.

He knocked the door back with a bang against the wall. In the flickers of dying firelight from the old stone fireplace, he saw a shadow move in the bed.

"Kasimir?" Josie's voice was sleepy. She sat up in bed, yawning. "Was that you yelling?"

Relief and joy rushed through him, so great it nearly brought him to his knees. Without a word, he sat down on the bed and pulled her into his arms. In the moonlight from the window, he saw her beautiful, precious face, her cheeks lined with creases from the pillow, her messy hair tumbling over her shoulders, auburn in the red glow from the fire's dying embers.

"What is it? What's wrong?"

Kasimir didn't answer. For long moments, he just sat on the bed, holding her. Closing his eyes, he inhaled the scent of vanilla and peaches in hair, felt the sweet softness of her body pressed against his own.

"Kasimir?" Her voice was muffled against his chest. He finally pulled back, gripping her shoulders as he looked down at her.

"Where are the bodyguards?" he said hoarsely. "Why are you alone?"

"Oh... That." To his surprise, she shrugged, then gave him a crooked grin. "They got in this big fight, arguing over which of them got to watch some huge sports event on the big screen in the basement and which poor slob would be stuck watching me. So I told them in Russian that I didn't need anyone watching me. I mean—" she gave a little laugh "—I've been sleeping on my own for a long time. My whole life. I mean—" she suddenly blushed, looking at him "—until quite lately." Drawing back, she looked at him. "You aren't mad, are you?" she said anxiously. "I promised them you wouldn't be mad."

"I will fire them all," Kasimir said fervently. Pulling her hard against his body, he pressed his lips to hers in a kiss that was pure and true and that he wished could last forever—but he feared would be their last.

This time, she was the one to pull away. "You don't really mean that," she said chidingly. "You can't fire them. They had to obey me. I'm your wife."

"Of course they had to obey you," he growled.

"Good," she sighed. She pressed her cheek against his chest, then sat up in sudden alarm. "The phone line got cut off when I tried to talk to Bree. Was she mad? Did you cut the deal with Vladimir? When will I see her?"

Kasimir looked down into her beautiful, trusting face, feeling heartsick. "She's safe and happy and you'll see her in three days." His jaw clenched, and he forced himself to say, "But there's something I need to tell you."

Josie shook her head, narrowing her eyes with a determined set of her chin. "I have something to tell you first."

"No—"

She covered his mouth with her small hand. She looked straight into his eyes. And she said the five words that for ten years, he'd never wanted to hear from any woman.

"I'm in love with you," Josie whispered.

With an intake of breath, he pulled back, his eyes wide. He looked at her face, pink in the warm firelight. "What did you say?" he choked out.

Josie's eyes were luminous as she looked up at

him with a trembling smile. Then she said the words again, and it was like the home he'd dreamed of his whole life. "I love you, Kasimir."

"But—you can't." He realized his body was shaking all over. "You don't."

"I do." Her eyes glowed like sunlight and Christmas and everything good he'd ever dreamed of. "I knew it last night, when you held me in your arms. And I had to tell you before I lost my courage. Because even if you're mean to me, even if you push me away, even if you divorce me and I never see you again..." She lifted her gaze to his. "I love you."

Standing up, Kasimir stumbled back from her. Pacing three steps, he stopped, clawing his hair back wildly as he faced her in the moonlight. "You're wrong. Sex can feel like love, especially the first time. When you don't have enough experience to know the difference..."

Pushing aside the quilts, she slowly stood up in her plaid flannel nightgown. "I know the difference." Her eyes pierced his. "Do you?"

His heart started to pound.

He didn't want to think about how being with Josie was so different from anything he'd ever experienced before. Couldn't. "Don't you understand what kind of man I am?" he said hoarsely. "I'm selfish. Ruthless. I've spent ten years trying to destroy my own brother! How can you love me?"

Coming towards him, she put her hand over his. "Because I do."

A tremble went through him then that he couldn't control. Outside, through the windows, the sky was turning lighter as dawn rose pink and soft. It was New Year's Day.

"You should hate me," he whispered. "I want you to hate me."

Reaching up, Josie cupped his cheek, her palm soft against the rough bristles of his jawline. "You don't have to be afraid."

He stiffened. "Afraid?"

"Of loving me back," she said quietly. She took a deep breath. "You want to love me. I think you already do. But you're afraid I'll hurt you or leave you. What will it take for you to see you have nothing to fear? I've never loved anyone before, but I know one thing. I will love you," she whispered, "for always."

Their eyes locked in the gray shadows of the bedroom. The icy wind rattled the window, and the fire crackled noisily.

"There. I'm done." Tears shone in her eyes as she gave him a trembling smile. "Now what did you want to tell me?"

And just like that, Kasimir suddenly knew.

He couldn't tell Josie the truth. Because he wanted her in his life. No, it was more than just wanting her.

He couldn't bear to let her go.

Kasimir's throat ached. But even if he lied to her now, he wouldn't be able to keep the truth from her for long. In three days, when he took her to Morocco for the exchange, she'd discover what he'd done. That he'd been keeping her prisoner all this time. Even she could not forgive that.

Unless…

Was there any way he could keep her as his wife? Any way he could keep her in his bed, with that innocent, passionate love still shining so brightly in her eyes?

Slowly, Kasimir lifted his hand to stroke the softness of her hair. "What I wanted to tell you is…" He took a deep breath. "I missed you."

Josie sighed in pleasure, closing her eyes, pressing her cheek against his chest in an expression that was protective, almost reverent.

In the warmth and comfort of her arms, Kasimir closed his stinging eyes against his own weakness for the lie. Then, in the wintry Russian dawn, against the cold blank slate of a brand-new year, he lowered his mouth to hers for a forbidden kiss. And then another. Until they were tangled together, and he was lost.

Josie had been feeling hurt, with an aching heart, when he'd left her in his tuxedo, to go to the New Year's Eve ball without her. Then she'd been struck by a thought so sudden and overwhelming that it had made her stand still.

Her husband, for all his wealth and power, was completely alone.

Josie couldn't imagine having no family, except a brother who was an enemy. She knew that Bree, for all her overbearing ways, still loved her fiercely. The two sisters had each other's backs—always. But who had Kasimir's back?

No one.

Who loved him on this wide, lonely earth?

Nobody.

Realizing this, Josie's wounded heart had abruptly stopped aching. The tears had disappeared. He had no one who believed in him—no one he could trust. No wonder he'd devoted his life to the success of a business that had never been his childhood dream, to earning money he didn't really need, and most of all—to destroying his only family. His brother.

No wonder his moral compass was so askew. No wonder, when they'd spent the night together in bed and she'd given him her heart, as well as her body, he hadn't known how to react.

But he'd never been loved as she could love him.

Kasimir expected her to stop caring about him the instant he did something cold or rude. Well, he didn't know the type of woman he was dealing with. Josie had been ignored and dismissed her whole life. She'd never once let that stop her from believing the best of people and giving them everything she could.

She knew Kasimir had darkness inside him. She accepted that it was part of him. But as long as he was honest with her, honorable and true, she didn't care. Everyone had flaws. She did. It wouldn't stop her from loving him, the only way she knew how to love someone.

All the way.

Josie loved him. Come what may.

At that simple decision, peace had come over her. The bodyguards, who'd been arguing over who would be stuck watching the crying woman instead of the two-hundred-inch projector screen in the basement, had been astonished when she'd suddenly stopped pacing and told them in clumsy Russian to go watch the game. She'd gone alone to the kitchen. She'd made herself some Russian tea. After speaking briefly to her sister, who sounded very shocked indeed that Josie had married Kasimir, she'd brushed her teeth, put on her nightgown and gone to bed. Rehearsing what she would tell him, she'd waited for her husband to come home.

She'd fallen asleep, but it didn't matter. She hadn't used a word of her little rehearsed speech anyway. She'd just taken one look at the gray bleak shadows on Kasimir's face, at the tight set of his shoulders, and spoken the truth from her heart.

Now, pulling back from his sudden hungry kiss, Josie looked at him. His eyes seemed haunted, tortured, dark as a midnight sea. But he cared for her. She could see it. Feel it. Reaching up, she cupped his cheek. He put his rough hand over hers, then pressed his lips to her palm in a lingering kiss so passionate that her soul thrilled inside her body.

And looking at him, she felt no more trembling fear. She felt only the absolute knowledge, down to her bones, that her love for him was meant to be.

This time, Kasimir was the one who was shaking, as if he felt her words of love like a physical blow. She tried to imagine what his life had been like for the last ten years, unloved and alone—never knowing what it was to be protected and sheltered by another human soul.

Starting today, and for the rest of his life, he would know. She would shelter him. Protect him.

Beside the bed, she pulled the black overcoat off his unresisting body. She removed his tuxedo jacket and dropped it to the floor. Pushing him to sit on the bed, she knelt and unlaced his black Italian leather shoes, then she reached up for his black tie.

He grabbed her wrist. "What are you doing?"

She exhaled, then leaned up, smiling through her tears.

"Let me show you," she whispered.

His eyes widened. His hand numbly released her.

Pulling off his tie, Josie undid the top button of his white tuxedo shirt, then the waistband of his black trousers. She removed all his clothes, one by one, then pushed him back against the bed. Looking down at him, she yanked her long nightgown up over her head. She kicked off her panties. For a split second, she shivered in the cool winter air as they stared at each other, both naked in the flickering firelight, against the misty gray dawn. Then she pulled the goose-down comforter over them.

Beneath the blanket was their own world. She wrapped her arms around his hard, shivering body, trying to warm them both. She kissed his forehead. Then his cheek. Then…

Suddenly, staying warm was not a problem. She felt hot, burning hot, with his naked skin against her own. She kissed him, clutching him to her, and a growl came from the back of his throat.

Putting his hands on both sides of her face, Kasimir kissed her back fiercely, possessively, almost violently. Rolling her body beneath him, he kissed slowly down her neck, running his hands over her naked skin as if it were silk. As if he wanted to explore every inch of her.

Insane, intoxicating need overwhelmed her. If he couldn't say the three words that she yearned to hear, she needed to feel his love for her.

"Take me," she whispered. "Now."

He sucked in his breath, searching her eyes. Then, gripping her hips, he pulled back, then thrust inside her, filling her so deeply, all the way to the heart.

She gasped, gripping his shoulders. He wrapped his arms around her, pressing his hard body against her own, and she felt the heat of his breath against her skin as he rode her slow and hard and deep. She cried out, clutching him to her. Drawing back, he looked straight into her eyes, holding her gaze as he plunged one last time, deep, so deep, that she shuddered all around him, as he shuddered inside her.

Afterward, tears ran down Josie's cheeks as she felt his strong arms around her, keeping cold winter away. *She loved him so.* And when Kasimir reached for her again a brief time later, to show her his love again and again, she knew that fairy tales were true. They had to be. Because even if he couldn't speak the words, he loved her. His body proved it.

They were in love. Weren't they? That meant everything would be all right. Didn't it? So they'd be together forever.

Wouldn't they?

Two and a half days later, in the rustic, dark-walled study of the country house, Kasimir dialed Bree Dalton's number with shaking hands. When she did not answer, he gritted his teeth and called a number he hadn't called for ten years. A number he knew by heart.

Kasimir had waited till the last possible moment to call. For three days now, he'd racked his brain to think of a way to keep both Josie and his revenge. But Bree expected her sister in exchange for the signed contract. There was no solution. Only a choice.

But such a choice. Kasimir had already sent his bodyguards with the luggage to the nearby private airport, where his jet was ready to take them to Marrakech. But then, five minutes ago, outside in the snow with Josie, watching her sparkling eyes as she made a snowman, he suddenly knew the answer.

He wanted Josie more than anything else. So the solution was screamingly obvious.

He would give up his revenge.

He would take Josie to some place where her sister and Vladimir would never find her.

He took a deep breath as Vladimir answered his phone.

"It's me," he ground out.

"Kasimir," his brother replied in a low voice. "About time."

Vladimir didn't sound surprised to hear from him. Strange. And stranger still that after ten years of silence, it seemed as if no time had passed between them. He sounded exactly the same.

"You might as well know, I tried to blackmail Bree," he said abruptly, "into signing your company over to me."

"She already told me," Vladimir replied. "Your plan to turn us against each other didn't work."

Kasimir stopped. "You already know? So what do you intend to do?"

"I am willing to make the trade."

He sucked in his breath. "You're willing to give up your billion-dollar company? For the sake of a woman who once lied to you?" His jaw hardened. Vladimir must really love Bree. "Too bad. I've changed my mind. I no longer have any intention of divorcing Josie, for any price. You can keep your stupid company. In fact…there's no reason for us ever to talk. Ever again."

"Kasimir, don't be a fool," his brother said tersely. "You can still—"

Kasimir turned his head as he heard Josie coming in from the snowy garden. He hung up, dropping his phone into his pocket.

"Why did you run off like that?" She was laughing, wearing a white hooded coat, halfcovered with snow. "We're not even done. The poor snowman only has one eye." Puppy-like, she tried to shake the snowflakes off her coat. Her eyes sparkled like a million bright winter days, and the sound of her laughter was like music. "Ah," she sighed. "I've missed winter!"

He'd never seen anything, or anyone, so beautiful. As he looked at her, his heart twisted with infinite longing.

And he realized: *he loved her*.

His eyes narrowed, and he knew he wouldn't let anyone take Josie away from him. He'd keep her. At any cost.

"I have something to tell you," he said softly. He pulled off her white hooded coat, covered with snow, off her shoulders and dropped it to the floor. "It's important."

Josie gave him a teasing, slow-rising smile. "Hmm. Knowing you…" She tilted her head, pretending to consider, then lifted an eyebrow. "Does that something involve a bed?"

"Ah. You know me well," he answered with a wicked grin. "But no." Growing more serious, he gently used the pads of his thumbs to wipe away the snowflakes from her creamy skin, and those tangled in her eyelashes. Looking down into her eyes, he saw eternity in those caramel-and-honey-colored depths. And he whispered the words in his heart. "I love you, Josie."

Her lips parted in shock. Tears filled her eyes as a sob escaped her. "You love me?"

He cupped her cheek. "Will you stay with me and be my wife?" He gave her a crooked, cocky smile, even as his hands trembled. "Not just now, but forever?"

"Forever," she breathed. A single tear streamed down her cheek. "Yes," she choked out. She threw her arms around him. "Oh, yes!"

He pulled back from her embrace to look down at her. "But there's just one thing." He looked down at her. "If you stay with me as my wife—you must never see Bree again."

"What?" She wiped her eyes with an awkward laugh. "What are you talking about?"

"I saw your sister with my brother at the ball. Laughing. Kissing. They are together now." He set his jaw. "So you must choose. Them…" He tucked back a long tendril of her hair and said in a low voice, "Or me."

Josie blinked fast. "Maybe if we all just talked together, we could…"

"No," he cut her off.

Josie stared at him, her brown eyes glittering. She swallowed, then whispered, "You can't ask this of me."

"I must." He pulled her into his arms. His hands moved to her back, getting tangled in her lustrous, damp brown hair. He kissed her temple, her cheek, her lips. "Choose me, Josie," he whispered against her skin. "Stay with me."

She trembled in his arms, uncertain. Knowing he'd asked her the deepest sacrifice of her life, he persuaded her in the only way he could. He lowered his mouth to hers, kissing her with his soul on his lips, holding nothing back. He kissed her with every bit of love and longing and passion in his heart, until even Kasimir was dizzy as the world seemed to spin around their embrace.

"Let me show you the world," he whispered. "Every day can be more exciting than the last. Choose me."

Her arms twisted around his shoulders as she sighed against his lips. "I can't..."

He kissed her again. In the distance, he dimly heard noises outside the dacha—the call of the birds, the crack of wood in the bare forest.

With a sob, Josie pulled away. A single tear fell unheeded down her cheek. "I love you both." She drew a deep breath like a shudder, then lifted her gaze and whispered, "But if I must choose, I choose you."

Kasimir's heart almost stopped in his chest.

Josie chose him.

It was a selfish thing he'd asked of her, he knew. Selfish? Unforgivable. And yet this amazing woman had chosen him. Over everything and everyone she'd ever loved. He got a lump in his throat. "Thank you, Josie," he said in a low voice. "I'll honor your sacrifice. For the rest of our lives...."

The outside door banged against the wall. Whirling around, Josie gasped, "Bree!"

As if in slow motion, Kasimir turned his head.

Vladimir and Bree stood in the open doorway.

"Josie." The slender blond woman ran quickly towards her younger sister. "Are you all right?"

"Of course I'm all right," Josie tried to reassure her. "You're the one who's been in trouble." She patted her sister's shoulders as if to be sure she was really there. "But are you okay?" she said anxiously. She scowled at Vladimir. "He didn't—hurt you?"

"Vladimir?" Bree looked astonished. "No. Never."

"What are you doing here?"

"We came to save you."

"Save me?" Looking bewildered, Josie looked at Kasimir with a smile then tilted her head. "Oh. You mean from my marriage." She sighed. "I knew you'd be upset I married Kasimir, but you don't need to worry. It started out as a business arrangement, yes, but now we're in love and..."

Her voice trailed off as she looked at the faces of

the others. Vladimir folded his arms, glowering at Kasimir. He stared back at his brother warily.

What's going on?" Josie breathed, looking bewildered.

Kasimir set his jaw. He'd been so close—so close to getting her away forever. But now he had no choice but to tell her *everything*—before the others did. He turned to her, his arms folded.

"There's something I need to tell you," he said tightly. "Something I need to explain."

"Go on," she said uncertainly.

He desperately tried to think of a way to make her understand, to forgive. "It was… I thought it was fate." He tightened his hands into fists at his sides. "When you fell into my lap."

He parted his lips to say more, then stopped.

"Kasimir threatened me on New Year's Eve," Bree stated. "He said if I didn't trick Vladimir into signing over his company, he would make sure I never saw you again!"

Josie gasped.

Her sister scowled. "I had to get the contract signed by midnight tonight, or Kasimir was going to make you disappear into the desert forever. Into his harem, he said!"

Josie's face went pale. "No," she breathed. She turned to him. "It's not true," she whispered. "Tell me it's not true. It's some kind of—misunderstanding between you and my sister. Tell me."

Kasimir's shoulders and jaw were so tense they

hurt as he looked down at her. "I was going to explain, the night I came back on New Year's Eve. Having you with me, when Bree was with Vladimir, it just seemed—well, I told myself I'd be a fool not to take advantage of the situation." He paused, then forced himself to continue. "I...I was the one who arranged for you and your sister to get jobs in Hawaii."

"You did!"

He gave a single terse nod. "I hoped to convince you to marry me. And I hoped Vladimir would see Bree."

"You mean you hoped I'd cause a scene," Bree retorted.

"Which you did," Vladimir murmured, giving her a wicked grin. She blushed.

"That's neither here nor there," she said primly.

But Josie's soft brown eyes didn't look away from Kasimir's face. "That's why you took me from Honolulu to Morocco?" The color had drained out of her rosy cheeks, leaving her skin white as Russian snow. "You weren't keeping me safe—you were keeping me hostage? To blackmail my sister?"

Kasimir's heart twisted in his chest. "Josie." He swallowed. "If you'll just let me explain...."

And again, she waited, still with a terrible, desperate hope in her eyes. As if there could be any way Kasimir could explain his actions that didn't make him a selfish monster. He took a deep breath. "I did do a terrible thing. But an hour ago, I called and told them the deal was off. I told Vladimir he could keep his company. All I wanted was you." Urgently, he grabbed her hands in his own and looked down at her. "Doesn't that mean something?" he said softly. "I called off the blackmail. For you."

For a moment, Josie's eyes glowed. For that split second, he thought it was all going to be all right.

Then her expression crumpled. "But you were going to separate me from my sister forever, rather than confess how you tried to blackmail her. You were going to force me to give her up, her friendship, her love, for the rest of my life, rather than tell me how you threatened her—with my *safety!*"

"I was afraid." Words caught in his throat. He felt her hands starting to slip away and he tried to grab them, hold on to them. "I was afraid you wouldn't understand. I couldn't take the risk you wouldn't forgive me...."

She pulled her hands away. "If even an hour ago, you'd confessed everything, I think even then I could have forgiven you," she whispered. "But not for th-this." Her teeth chattered. "You d-demanded that I make that horrible choice. When it was never necessary. Even knowing what it would cost me!"

"I'm sorry," he said in a low voice.

Her eyes widened, then narrowed. "You never loved me," she choked out. "Not if you could do that."

Desperately, he took a step towards her. "It was the only way I could keep you!"

She flinched. Closing her eyes, she exhaled. "I always wondered why a man like you would be interested in a woman like me. Now I know." She opened her eyes, and tears spilled over her lashes. "I was just a possession to you. Someone to be married for the sake of land in Alaska, then traded for your brother's company. Then kept at your whim, as what? Your mistress, your sex slave?"

"My wife!"

"You never thought of...of *me*. How I would feel. You either didn't think about it, or you didn't care."

"It's not true!" With a deep breath, he said, "Yes, I tried to use you to get revenge on my brother. But everything changed, Josie, when I...I fell in love with you."

She stared at him. Turning away with a sob, she pressed her face against her sister's shoulder.

"Please," Kasimir whispered, taking a step towards her. "Doesn't it mean anything that I gave up what I wanted most—the company that should have been mine?"

"You don't have to give it up." Vladimir stepped between them, his face grave. Reaching into his coat, he pulled out a white page. "Here it is."

For an instant, Kasimir stared blankly at the page. He took it from his brother's hand. Looking down, he sucked in his breath. "It's the contract I gave Bree." He looked up in shock. "It transfers your shares in Xendzov Mining to me. You signed it."

"Let this be the end," Vladimir said. "I was

wrong to force you out of our company ten years ago. I was angry, and humiliated, and my pride wanted vengeance. But I was the only one to blame. So take back what I owe you, with interest. Take it all. And let this be the end of our war."

Kasimir's mouth was dry. "You're just giving it to me?" His voice was hoarse. "Just like that?"

"Just like that."

"A lifetime's work. You're throwing it away?"

Vladimir's forehead creased. "I'm trading it. For the happiness of the woman I love. The woman who will soon be my wife." His blue eyes, the same shade as Kasimir's own, were filled with regret as he said softly, "And to make amends to the little brother I always loved, but have sometimes treated very badly."

A lump rose in Kasimir's throat.

"I should have waited for you," Vladimir said in a low voice, "all those days we walked to school in the snow." Glancing behind him, he gave a sudden snort. "And I should have listened when you said Bree Dalton was a wicked creature, not to be trusted…"

"Hey," she protested behind him.

Lifting a dark eyebrow, Vladimir gave her a sensual smile. "You know you're wicked. Don't try to deny it." Then he looked back to Kasimir, his expression serious. "I was wrong to cut you out of my life," he said humbly. "Forgive me, brother."

Kasimir's world was spinning. He gripped the

contract like a life raft. "You can't mean it," he said. "You've put your whole life into Xendzov Mining. How can you just surrender? How can you let me win?"

"For the same reason that, an hour ago, you were willing to let it go." Vladimir gave a crooked smile. "I've won a treasure far greater than any company. The life I always wanted. With the woman I always loved. You reunited us in Hawaii. And I have you to thank for that."

"I was trying to hurt you," he said hoarsely.

His older brother's smile lifted to a grin. "You did me the biggest favor of my life. Now you're taking the mining company off my hands, I'm off to Honolulu. I've just bought the Hale Ka'nani resort for Bree."

"You did what?"

"Oh, Bree," Josie breathed, clutching her sister's arm. "Just like you always dreamed!"

"I dreamed of running a little bed-and-breakfast by the sea." Bree's lips quirked as she looked at Vladimir. "Trust you to buy me a hundred-million-dollar hotel for my birthday!"

"It was way easier than trying to buy you jewelry," he said, and she laughed.

Kasimir's throat hurt as he looked down at the signed contract in his hand. He had the company he'd always wanted. He'd soon have Josie's land in Alaska. He even had his brother's apology.

He'd won.

And yet, he suddenly didn't feel that way. He looked past Vladimir and Bree to the only thing that mattered.

"Can you forgive me, Josie?" he whispered. "Can you?"

She looked up from Bree's shoulder. Her cheeks were streaked with tears, her face pale.

His heart fell to his feet. He tried to smile. "It's in the marriage vows, isn't it? You have to forgive me. For better, for worse. Can't we just agree that you're the better, and I'm the worse—"

Josie held up her hand, cutting him off. He stared at her, feeling sick as he waited for the verdict. She'd never looked so beautiful to him as she did at that moment, when he knew all he deserved was for her to walk out the door.

"I was willing to give up everything." She sounded almost bewildered. She put her hand to her forehead. "*Everything*. How could I have been so stupid?" She looked up, her eyes wide. "I was willing to give up everything for you. My family, my home, my life—everything that makes me *me*. For a romantic dream! For *nothing!*"

Kasimir's heart stopped in his chest. "It's not a dream. Josie—"

"Stop it!" Her sweet, lovely face hardened as her eyes narrowed. "It *was* a dream. I knew you were ruthless. I knew you were selfish. But I didn't know you were a liar and more heartless than I ever imagined!"

"I'm sorry," he whispered. He swallowed. "If you'll just—"

"No!" She cut him off every bit as ruthlessly as he'd once done to her, again and again. He flinched, remembering. She took a deep breath, and her voice turned cold. "As soon as my land in Alaska is transferred to your name, there's only one thing I want from you."

"Anything," he said desperately.

Josie lifted her chin, and for the first time, her brown eyes held a sliver of ice. He saw her soul there, what he'd done to her, in a kaleidoscope of blue and green and shadows, glittering like a frost-covered forest, frozen as midnight. "I want a divorce."

CHAPTER TEN

ALMOST FOUR WEEKS later, Josie watched her sister and Vladimir get married in a twilight beachside ceremony in Hawaii.

Seeing their happiness as they spoke their wedding vows, a lump rose in Josie's throat. The sun was setting over the ocean as they stood barefoot in the sand, the surf rushing over their feet. Bree wore a long white dress, Vladimir a white button-down shirt and khakis, and they both were decked in colorful fresh-flower leis. As the newly married couple kissed to the scattered applause of friends and family surrounding them on the beach, Josie felt a hard twist in her chest. She told herself she was crying because she was so happy Bree had found love at last.

Josie had filed for divorce the day before.

When her lawyer had called yesterday morning to tell her that the land in Alaska now officially belonged to Kasimir, Josie had thanked him, and told him to file papers for their divorce.

She'd had no choice. She'd given Kasimir all her

trust and faith, and he'd still selfishly asked her to make a sacrifice that would have destroyed her—a sacrifice that didn't even have to be made, if he'd just been honest enough to confess!

But her heart was breaking. She'd loved him so. She loved him still.

She'd never forget when Kasimir had told her he loved her on that cold winter day in Russia. She'd thought she would die of happiness. Now, Josie looked down, her tears dripping like rain into the bouquet of flowers she held as matron of honor.

Love. Kasimir hadn't known the meaning of the word. He'd never loved her. All the time she'd spent worshipping him, all the sunny optimistic hopes she'd had that she could change him—what a joke. She felt like a fool. Because she was one.

Blinking fast, Josie watched Bree's fluffy white puppy happily entwining herself around the happy couple, before running up and down the beach in pure doggy joy. She'd been like Snowy, she thought. Like Kasimir's slavishly adoring pet, waiting by the door with his slippers in her mouth. Pathetic.

And now he'd gotten what he wanted all along. His brother's company and his apology. Seducing Josie had just been a way for the notoriously ruthless womanizer to pass the time.

Everything changed, Josie. She had the sudden memory of his haunted eyes. *When I...I fell in love with you.*

She squeezed her eyes shut. No. She didn't believe it. Kasimir was just a man who didn't know how to lose, that was all. He'd wanted to keep her, but not enough to pursue her back to Hawaii. He'd let her go, and had never bothered to contact her since. If he'd loved her, he would have tried to fight for her. He hadn't.

Should she still tell him?

Josie shivered. Still standing in the surf on the beach, surrounded by applauding friends and her new husband, Bree looked at her sister with worried eyes.

Straightening her shoulders, Josie forced her lips into a quick, encouraging smile. She couldn't let Bree know. Not yet.

She exhaled as the group started walking back up the beach towards the Hale Ka'nani for the reception.

Bree was working sixteen-hour days as the new owner of the five-star resort and loving every minute of it. Her first act had been to double the salaries of the hotel's housekeepers. The second was to fire the vendors who'd been double-charging their accounts. Employee morale had skyrocketed since the tyrannical reign of their hated ex-boss, Greg Hudson, had ended.

And both sisters' futures were brighter than Josie had ever imagined. Thanks to Vladimir, there were no longer angry men demanding that Josie and her sister repay their dead father's debts. Without a company to run, he had pronounced himself—at thirty-

five—to be retired. But Bree confided she thought
he missed working. "Not for the money. But for
the fun."

Fun? Josie had shaken her head. But who was she
to judge what made people happy? Life was wher-
ever your heart was.

Her own life had become unrecognizable. She'd
left Honolulu a poor housekeeper, desperate, broke
and completely insecure. Now, she'd started spring
classes at the University of Hawaii, and instead of
living in a dorm, she had her own luxurious beach
villa, right next to her sister's at the Hale Ka'nani.
She'd finally gotten her driver's license—and she'd
bought herself a brand-new, snazzy red two-seater
convertible. For which she'd paid cash.

But she was going to have to return the convertible to the dealer. And see if she could exchange it
for something that had room for another passenger
in the back.

Josie put her hand over her belly in wonder. As
the small, intimate wedding reception began in the
open-air hotel bar, and Bree and Vladimir cut their
wedding cake together beneath the twinkling fairy
lights in the night, she still couldn't quite believe
it. How could she be pregnant? She blushed. Well,
she knew, but she'd never thought it could happen.

Pregnant. With Kasimir's baby.

A soft smile traced her lips. She was starting to
get used to the idea. Maybe Kasimir didn't love her.

Maybe Josie's heart would never recover. But he'd still given her the most precious gift of all.

A child.

No one knew yet. She was afraid of what Bree would say. At twenty-two, Josie was young to be a mother. Other women her age were worried about the next frat party or calculus test.

But thanks to Kasimir, there was at least one thing Josie would never need to worry about: money. The day after she left Russia, before he'd even gotten the land in Alaska, he'd placed an amount in her bank account that she still couldn't even quite comprehend, because it had so many zeroes at the end.

"Josie? Is everything okay?"

Looking up, she saw Bree in front of her. Her long blond hair tumbled over her flower lei and white cotton dress as she looked at her sister with concern.

"You look beautiful," Josie whispered. "I'm so happy for you."

"Cut the crap. What's wrong?"

Trust her sister to see right through her. Forcing her lips into a smile, she said, "It's your wedding. We can talk later."

"We'll talk now. Is it Kasimir?" Bree's gaze sharpened. "Has he tried to contact you?"

"Contact me?" Josie gave a low, harsh laugh. "No."

Bree scowled. Then grabbing Josie's hand, she pulled her out of the outdoor bar and into a quiet, dark gazebo in the shadowy garden overlooking the cliff. "Look, you're better off without him," she said urgently. "Plenty of other fish in the sea. You'll find someone really great, who appreciates you—"

Josie flinched. "I know," she quickly said to end the horror of the conversation.

"Then what?"

She paused. "Let's talk about it a different day. After your honeymoon."

"Honeymoon?" Bree grinned. "I'm living in Hawaii, in my dream job, with the man I love! I'll be on honeymoon for the rest of my life!"

"I'm so happy for you," Josie repeated, ignoring the ache in her throat. Resisting the urge to wipe her eyes, she looked down at the wet, soft grass beneath her feet. "After years of taking care of me, you deserve a lifetime of love and joy."

"Hey." Bree lifted her chin gently. "So do you. And I can't be happy until I know what's going on."

Josie blinked back tears, trying to smile. "You've always been a mother hen."

"Always." Her older sister looked into her eyes. "So you might as well tell me what's going on, or I'll be pecking at you all night."

Josie took a deep breath.

"I'm...I'm pregnant," she whispered.

Her sister gasped. "Pregnant? Are you sure?"

She nodded.

Bree took a deep breath, then visibly gained control of herself. "It's Kasimir's." It was a statement, not a question.

"He doesn't know." Josie looked away, blinking back tears. "And I don't know if I should tell him."

"Are you going to keep the baby?"

Josie whirled to face her. "Of course I am!"

"You could consider adoption…"

"I'm not giving up my baby!"

"You're just so young." Bree's hazel eyes were full of emotion. "You have no idea how hard it is. What you're in for."

"I know." Josie swallowed. "You were only six when Mom died, and eighteen when we lost Dad. All these hard years, you've taken care of me…"

"I loved every minute."

Josie looked at her skeptically.

"All right," Bree allowed with a grin, "maybe not every *single* minute." She paused. "I was so scared at times for you."

"Because I was always screwing up," Josie said sadly.

"You?" Her sister's lips parted, then she shook her head fiercely beneath the colored lights of the wooden gazebo. "I was scared I would fail you. Scared I'd never be the respectable, honest, careful mother you deserved, no matter how hard I tried."

Something cracked in Josie's heart.

"That's why you hovered over me?" she whispered. "I thought I was a burden to you, forcing you to give up ten years to look after me."

"I felt like the luckiest big sister in the world to have a sweet kid like you to look after." Bree took a deep breath. "But you don't know what it's like to raise a child. To fear for them every moment." She looked down at the wet hem of her white dress. "To pray that your own stupid mistakes won't hurt the sweet, innocent one you love so, so much."

"You worried you might make a mistake?" Josie said in amazement. Shaking her head, she patted her sister's shoulder. "You gave me a wonderful childhood that I'll never forget." Josie bit her lip, and forced herself to say what she'd been too afraid to say before. "But I'm all grown up now. You don't need to be my mother any more. Just be my sister. My friend." She looked at her. "Just be my baby's aunt."

Bree stared at her. Then, bursting into tears, she pulled Josie into her arms, hugging her tightly.

"You'll be a wonderful mother," she choked out, wiping her eyes. "You're the strongest person I know. You've always been so fearless. You've never been afraid of anything."

"Me?" Josie cried.

Bree gave a laugh, shaking her head as she smiled through her tears. "The stunts you used to pull. Snowboarding in Alaska. While I was hesitating over the safest way, or worrying about the risks, you'd just fly straight past me, head-first. And that's how you love." She looked at Josie. "You're still in love with him, aren't you?"

Josie's lips parted. Then, wordlessly, she nodded. "Are you going to tell him? About the baby?"

"Should I?"

With a rueful little smile, Bree shook her head. "That's a choice that only you can make." She paused. "Because you're right, Josie. You're all grown up."

Josie hugged her sister tight, then pulled away, wiping her eyes. "I do love him. But he doesn't love me. I know now that he's never going to come for me. I'll never see him again."

"I don't know about that." There was a strange expression on Bree's face as she looked at a point above her ear.

Frowning, Josie turned around.

And saw Kasimir standing behind her, just outside the dark gazebo, in the warm Hawaiian night.

Kasimir's heart was thudding in his throat.

Josie's big brown eyes looked up at him in shock, as if she thought she was dreaming. She was chewing her pink bottom lip in an adorable way, wearing a simple pink cotton bridesmaid's dress, with her soft brown hair hanging in waves over her bare, tanned shoulders.

So beautiful. So incredibly beautiful. Seeing her face, breathing the same air, almost close enough to touch—Kasimir felt alive again for the first time since she'd left him. Especially when he saw she was still wearing her wedding ring.

Kasimir ran his thumb over his own gold wedding band. He'd never taken it off. It had become a part of him.

And so had she.

When he'd burst into the wedding reception, he'd immediately looked for Josie. Instead, he'd seen his brother standing near the bar. It had taken all of Kasimir's courage to tap him on the shoulder.

Still laughing at a friend's joke, Vladimir had turned around. The smile dropped from his face. "Kasimir," he whispered. "I didn't expect you."

"Then you shouldn't have sent me an invitation."

"No—that's not what I meant. I—"

"It's all right. I know what you meant. And until a few hours ago, I didn't know I was coming either." Reaching into the pocket of his jacket, Kasimir pulled out the contract. He pushed it into his brother's hand. "I can't take this. I don't want it."

His brother stared down at the signed contract now in his hand. "Why not?" he said faintly.

Kasimir blinked fast. "The truth is, I never really cared about taking over your company."

His brother snorted. "You gave a damned good impression."

Kasimir tilted his head and gave a low chuckle. "All right. Maybe I did want it. But what I wanted even more," he said in a low voice, swallowing against the ache in his throat, "was to have my brother back." He lifted his eyes. "I've missed you. I don't want to run your company. But..." He paused.

"A merger… We could run Xendzov Mining and Southern Cross together. As partners."

Vladimir stared at him. "Partners?"

"We'd have the second-largest mining company in the world. With your assets in the northern hemisphere, and mine in the southern…. We could dominate. Win. Together."

Vladimir blinked, his eyes dazed. "You'd give me a second chance? You'd trust me with your company? After the way I betrayed you?"

Kasimir gave him a crooked smile. "Yeah."

"Why?"

"Because we're brothers. But no more big-brother little-brother stuff. From now on, we're equals." He tilted his head, quirking a dark eyebrow. "What do you say?" Nervously, Kasimir held out his hand. "Will you be my business partner? Will you be my brother again?"

Vladimir stared at him for a long moment. Then he pushed his hand aside roughly.

Kasimir sucked in his breath.

His brother suddenly pulled him against his chest in a bear hug. His voice was muffled. "I've missed you. What do I say? Hell, yes. To all of it."

When the hug ended, both brothers turned away.

"Sand in my eyes," Kasimir muttered, wiping them with his hand.

"Stupid wind. Lifting sand from the beach." Wiping his own eyes, Vladimir cleared his throat in the windless night, then looked back at him and smiled, with his eyes still red. "From now on, we're equals. Through and through."

Kasimir snorted. "About time you figured that out."

"And by the way, your timing couldn't be better. Thanks for coming to save me. Turns out I'm no good at running a hotel." He gave a sudden grin. "This will save my wife the trouble of firing me."

Kasimir laughed. "Although she might miss you when you start commuting to Russia on a daily basis."

"Hmm." He grew thoughtful. "About that…"

The brothers spoke for a few minutes, and then Kasimir sighed. "I am sorry I missed your wedding."

"So am I." Vladimir punched him on the shoulder. "But having you back is the best wedding present any man could ask for." He lifted an eyebrow with a grin. "Though something tells me you didn't just come here for wedding cake. Or even a business deal."

"You're right." Kasimir took a deep breath. "Where is she, Volodya?"

At the use of his old nickname, Vladimir's eyes glistened. "Sorry," he said gruffly. "Sand again." He gestured towards a nearby cliff. "There. Talking to my wife."

Kasimir had looked past the outdoor bar to a gazebo, strung with colorful lights, on the edge of a cliff. He saw a moving shadow. *Josie*. At last! He'd turned to go, then stopped, facing his brother. He'd said in a low voice, "I'm glad we're friends again."

"Friends?" Vladimir's smile had lifted to a grin. "We're not friends, man. We're *brothers*."

Kasimir was glad and grateful beyond words that after ten years of estrangement, he and Vladimir were truly brothers again. But even that, as important as it was, wasn't the reason he'd flown for almost twenty-four hours straight from St. Petersburg across the North Atlantic to Alaska, and then across the endless Pacific to Hawaii.

Now, Kasimir took a deep breath as he looked down at Josie, facing him beneath the gazebo in the moonswept night. At the bottom of the cliff, he could hear the ocean waves crashing against the shore, but it was nothing compared to the roar of his own heart.

"What—what are you doing here?" Josie stammered. The music of her sweet, warm voice traveled through his body like electricity.

"My brother invited me to the wedding."

"You missed it," she said tartly.

"I know." He'd known he was too late when from the window of his plane, he'd seen the red sunset over Oahu. But the lights of Honolulu had still sparkled like diamonds in the center of the sunset's red fire, against the black water. Like magic. Because he knew Josie was there. "But the real question is," he whispered, "am I too late with you?"

Josie's lips parted.

Looking between her sister and Kasimir, Bree cleared her throat. "Um. I think I hear my husband calling me."

She hurried away from the gazebo, her wedding gown flying behind her. And for that alone, Kasimir could have forgiven her anything.

Turning, Josie started to follow. Kasimir grabbed her arm. "Please don't go."

"Why?" She looked at him. "What could we possibly have to talk about?"

"Vladimir and I worked through things," he said haltingly. He gave an awkward smile. "In fact, we've decided to combine our companies. Be partners."

Her jaw dropped. "You did?"

"I was in Alaska this morning, at the homestead. I had everything I ever wanted. And I suddenly realized something."

"What?" she whispered.

He looked at her. "I realized there's no point in having everything," he said softly, "if you can't share it with people you love."

Josie looked at him, her eyes wide. Swallowing, she looked away. "I'm happy you and your brother are friends again."

"Not friends." Kasimir grinned, remembering. *"Brothers."*

Josie looked at him, her eyes luminous and deep. "I'm glad," she said softly. Then she looked down. "But that doesn't have anything to do with me. Not anymore."

Kasimir knew his whole life depended on his next words. "He's not the reason I came back to Honolulu, Josie."

She looked up. "He's not?"

He shook his head, then looked down wryly at his dark wrinkled suit, white shirt and blue tie. "Do you know I haven't changed clothes for twenty-four hours?" He loosened his tie, then pulled it off. "When my lawyer said the land in Alaska was finally mine, I left St. Petersburg straight from the office. All I could think was I wanted to go home." His lips twisted. "But all I saw in Alaska was a rickety old cabin, piles of snow and a silent forest. It wasn't home." Looking straight into her eyes, he whispered, "Because it wasn't you."

Josie looked up at him, not even trying to hide the tears spilling over her lashes.

With a trembling hand, he reached out and brushed a tear from her cheek. "You're the home I've been trying to find for my whole life, Josie. You're my home."

"Then why did you let me go so easily?" she whispered.

Kasimir took a deep breath, closing his eyes, allowing the warm air to expand his lungs. "After you left," he said in a low voice, "I tried to convince myself I'd won. Then I tried to convince myself that you deserved a better man than me. Which you do. But this morning, in Alaska, I realized something that changed everything."

"What?" she faltered.

He looked straight into her eyes. "I can be that man." He took her hand in his own, and when she didn't pull it away he tightened his grasp, overwhelmed with need. "I can be the man who will mow the lawn by your white picket fence," he vowed. "The man who will be by your side forever. Worshipping you. For the rest of your life."

"But how can I believe you?" Josie wiped her eyes. "Our whole marriage was based on a lie. How can I ever give you my whole heart again?"

Kasimir stared at her, his heart pounding. He finally shook his head. "I don't know." He gave a low laugh, running his hand through his dark, tousled hair. "I wouldn't blame you for telling me to go to hell. In fact, I sort of figured you would."

"Then why come all this way?"

"Because you had to know what was in my heart," he whispered. "I had to tell you how you changed me. Forever. You made me want to be the idealistic, loyal person I once was. The man I was born to be."

Covering her face with her hands, she wept.

Falling on his knees before her, Kasimir wrapped his arms around her. "I'm so sorry I tried to separate you and your sister, Josie. I was selfish and I was a coward. Losing you was the one thing I thought I couldn't face."

He felt her stiffen, then slowly, her hand rose to

stroke his hair. It was the single sweetest touch of his life.

Kasimir looked up, his eyes hot with unshed tears. "But I should have thought of you first. Put *you* first. Now, all I want is for you to be happy. Whether you choose to be with me. Or—" he swallowed "—without—"

"Shut up." She put her finger to his lips, and his voice choked off. She said slowly, "I've learned I can live without you."

Kasimir's heart cracked inside his chest. He'd lost her. She was going to send him away, back into the bleak winter.

"But I've also learned," Josie whispered, "that I don't want to." Her brown eyes were suddenly warm, like the sky after a sudden spring storm. "I tried to stop loving you. But once I love someone, I love for life." Her lips lifted in a trembling smile. "I'm stubborn that way."

"Josie," he breathed, rising to his feet. He cupped her face, searching her gaze. "Does this mean you'll be my wife? This time for real?"

Reaching up, she said through her tears, "Yes. Oh, yes."

"You better make her happy!" Bree yelled. They turned in surprise to see Vladimir and his bride standing amid the flowers beyond the gazebo. Bree's eyes were shining with tears as she sniffed. "You'd better…"

"I will," Kasimir said simply. He turned back

to Josie and vowed with all his heart, "I will make you happy. It's all I will do. For the rest of my life."

And he lowered his head to kiss her, not caring that Bree and Vladimir stood three yards away from them, with all the partygoers of the wedding reception behind.

Let them look, he thought. *Let all the world see.*

Taking Josie tenderly in his arms, Kasimir kissed her with all the passion and promise of a lifetime. When he finally pulled away, she pressed her cheek against him with a contented sigh, and they stood together, holding each other in the moonswept night.

He could get used to Hawaii, he thought. In the distance, he heard the loud roar of the surf against the shore. He heard the wind through the palm trees, heard the cry of night birds soaring across the violet sky. And above it all, he heard the pounding of his own beating, living heart—his heart which, now and forever, was hers.

"I wish we could stay here," Josie said softly, for his ears only. She looked back at the other couple. "That we could live nearby, and all our children could someday play together on the beach…"

"About that…" Thinking of the decision he and his brother had just made, to build the world headquarters of their merged companies right here in Honolulu, Kasimir looked down at her with a mischievous grin. "I have a surprise for you."

"A surprise, huh?" Tears glistened in Josie's eyes

as she shook her head. A smile like heaven illuminated her beautiful face. "Just wait until you hear the one I have for you."

EPILOGUE

THE DAY JOSIE placed their newborn daughter in her husband's arms was the happiest day of her life, after eight months of joyful days.

All right, so her pregnancy hadn't been exactly easy. She'd been sick her first trimester, and for the last trimester, she'd been placed on hospital bed rest. But even that hadn't been so bad, really. She'd made friends with everyone on her hospital floor, from Kahealani and Grace, the overnight nurses who were always willing to share candy, to Karl, the head janitor who told riveting stories about his time as a navy midshipman with a girl in every port.

The world was full of friends Josie just hadn't met yet, and in those rare times when there was no one around, she always had plenty of books to read. Fun books, now. No more textbooks. She'd made it through spring semester, but now college was indefinitely on hold.

The truth was, Josie didn't really mind. Her real life—her real happiness—was right here. Now. Living with Kasimir in their beach villa, newly redecorated complete with a white picket fence.

Now, Josie smiled up from her hospital bed at Kasimir's awed, terrified, loving face as he held his tiny sleeping daughter for the first time.

"Need any help?"

"No." He gulped. "I think."

Looking at her husband holding their baby, tears welled up in Josie's eyes. They were a family. Kasimir loved working with his brother as partners in their combined company, Xendzov Brothers Corp. But for both princes, the way they did business had irrevocably changed. They still wanted to be successful, but the meaning of success had changed. "I want to make a difference in the world," Kasimir had said to her wistfully, lying beside her in the hospital bed last week. "I want to make the world a better place."

Josie hit him playfully with a pillow. "You do. Every time you bring me a slice of cake."

"No, I mean it." He'd looked at her out of the corner of his eye. "I was thinking…we could put half our profits into some kind of medical foundation for children. Maybe sell the palace in Marrakech for a new hospital in the Sahara." He stopped, looking at her. He said awkwardly, "What do you think?"

"So what's stopping you?" With a mock glare, she tossed his own words back at him. "The only one stopping you is *you*."

"Really? You wouldn't miss it?"

She snorted. "We don't need more money, or another palace." She thought of little Ahmed breaking his leg on the sand dune, far from medical care. "I love your hospital idea. And the foundation, too."

He looked down at her fiercely. "And I love you." Cupping her face, he whispered, "You're the best, sweetest, most beautiful woman in the world."

Nine months pregnant and feeling ungainly as a whale, having gained fifty extra pounds on banana bread, watermelon and ice cream, Josie had snorted a laugh, even as she looked at him tenderly. "You're so full of it."

"It's true," Kasimir had insisted, and then he kissed her until he made her believe he was an honest man.

Josie smiled. Kasimir always knew what to say. The only time she'd ever seen him completely without words was when she'd told him she was pregnant that night of Vladimir and Bree's wedding. At first, he'd just stared at her until she asked him if he needed to sit down—then, with a loud whoop and a holler, he'd pulled her into his arms.

With the divorce cancelled, he'd still insisted on remarrying her and doing it right, with their family in attendance. He'd actually suggested that they wed immediately, poaching Bree and Vladimir's half-eaten wedding cake, and grabbing the minister yawning at the bar. But rather than steal her sister's thunder, Josie had gotten him to agree to a compromise.

Tearing up the pre-nup, they'd married three days later, at dawn, on the beach. The ceremony had been simple, and as they'd spoken vows to love, cherish and honor each other for the rest of their lives, the brilliant Hawaiian sun had burst through the clouds like a benediction.

Then, of course, this being Hawaii, the clouds had immediately poured rain, forcing the five of them—Josie, Kasimir, Bree, Vladimir and the minister—to take off at a run for the shelter of the resort, with their leis trailing flower petals behind them. And once at the hotel, Josie had discovered the ten-tiered wedding cake her husband had ordered her—enough for a thousand or two people, covered with white buttercream flowers and their intertwined initials.

Her husband's sweet surprise was the most delicious cake of her life. Good thing too. Remembering, she gave a sudden grin. They were still eating wedding cake out of their freezer.

Josie glanced through the window in the door of her private room in the Honolulu hospital. In the hallway, she could see Bree pacing back and forth, a phone to her ear, telling Vladimir the happy news of the birth. Vladimir was still in St. Petersburg, finalizing the company's move to Honolulu. They were a very high-powered couple. Bree was having the time of her life running the Hale Ka'nani resort, which was already up in profits, having become newly popular with tourists from Japan and Australia. Vladimir and Bree did hope to start a family someday, but for now, they were having too much fun working.

Not Josie, though. All she wanted was right here. She looked at Kasimir and their daughter. Right now. A home. A husband. A family.

"Am I doing this right?" Kasimir said anxiously, his shoulders hunched and stiff as he cradled his baby daughter.

She snorted, leaning forward to stroke the baby's cheek with one hand. "You're asking me? It's not like I have more experience."

"I'm a little nervous," he confessed.

"You?" she teased. "Scared of an eight-pound baby?"

"Terrified." He took a deep breath. "I've never been a father before. What if I do something wrong?"

She put her hand on his forearm. "It won't matter." Tears spilled over her lashes as she smiled, loving him so much her heart ached with it. "You're the perfect father for her, because you love her." She looked down at the sleeping newborn in his arms. "And Lois Marie loves you already."

Kasimir's eyes crinkled. "Lulu is the best baby in the world," he agreed, using their baby's nickname. They'd named her after the mother Josie had never known. The mother who, along with her father, she would always remember. Josie would honor them both by being true to her heart. By singing the song inside her.

Holding hands, Kasimir and Josie smiled at their perfect little daughter, marveling at her soft dark hair, at her tiny hands and plump cheeks.

Then a new thought occurred to Josie, and she suddenly looked up in alarm. "What if I'm the one who doesn't know how to be a mother?" she asked.

"You?" Her husband gave a laugh that could properly be described as a guffaw. "Are you out of your mind? You'll be the best mother who ever lived." Cradling their tiny baby, securely nestled in the crook of his arm, he reached out a hand to cup Josie's cheek. "And I promise you," he whispered, "for the rest of my life, even if I make a mistake here or there, I'll love you both with everything I've got. And if I screw up, or if we fight, I'll always be the first to say I'm sorry." He looked at her. "I give you my word."

Reaching up, Josie wrapped her hand around his head, tangling her fingers in his dark hair. "Your word of honor?"

His eyes were dark. "Yes."

She took a deep breath.

"Show me," she whispered.

And as Kasimir lowered his head to hers, proving his words with a long, fervent kiss, Josie felt his vow in her heart like bright sun in winter. And she knew their bold, fearless life as a family, complicated and crazy and oh, so happy, had just begun.

* * * * *